THE ONE EYED BRIDE

Book III | The Ruthenian Chronicle

Rebecca Ganesh

ISBN-13: 979-8-9997679-4-3 (ebook), 979-8-9997679-5-0 (paperback)

Cover design by: Art Painter
Library of Congress Control Number: 2018675309
Printed in the United States of America

CONTENTS

CHAPTER 1

The Likho

The *likho* rubbed her tendrils together in delight. She had found the perfect victim to wrap her limbs around, to curse with a lovely dose of bad luck. The woman was hunched and wizened with age. She wore a shawl over her plain, green *rubakha* and walked with a cane carved from black hawthorne. She moved slowly as she collected the mushrooms that ringed the bases of the trees. The *likho* opened her mouth in a broad, toothy smile, imagining how she might make the cane slip from the woman's hand. Or perhaps make the old woman trip on a raised root. Or many other bad luck happenings.

The *likho* slipped from the cover of the trees and darted like a shadow across the narrow clearing, the wind catching in her dark limbs. She coiled her tendrils around the old woman's neck.

Most humans could not tell when a *likho* cursed them, when a *likho* wrapped themselves around their neck. Not until misfortunes began to pile up. But the old woman was different. She stiffened as the *likho* buried her face into the old woman's floral-patterned headscarf.

Then, the old woman lifted her hand, her sleeve falling back to reveal an arm covered in dozens of tattooed runes. Her hand moved in sharp strokes, drawing a glowing sigil in the air. The *likho* yelped as fiery red pain lanced through her limbs; and she fell stunned into the decaying pine needles. The old woman – a *ved'ma*, a witch – drew another rune in the air before the *likho* could move. It crackled with red light and smelled faintly of mint.

The *likho*'s grew heavy, her body pressing into the forest

floor. She lifted a shaking tendril– No, she no longer had tendrils for limbs. Instead, a human hand reached up as though to block her from a strike. The *likho* recoiled. She felt herself. No longer was she made of shadows and the cold just before dawn. No, now she had a body. A warm, bony, bloody, *human* body. She felt her face. She still only had one eye.

The old woman tapped her cane against the ground with a soft *thud*. Looking at her with a new eye, the *likho* burned in embarrassment. She should have recognized the *ved'ma* immediately. This was no ordinary old woman with wispy iron-gray hair and a wrinkled face, but Baba Les, who was both a powerful *ved'ma* and a spirit of the forest.

"You picked the wrong witch to give bad luck." Baba Les drew another sigil in the air. This one glittered black and then a slinky, black rope appeared in the old woman's hands. Like a snake, the rope slithered and curled around the *likho*'s wrists. For a moment, it even looked like it had grown scales. "Come now."

The rope around the *likho*'s wrists burned, and she quickly stood up. She was uneasy on her human feet at first, but it did not matter. Drawing another rune in the air, Baba Les summoned a portal. Taking her cane, her basket of mushrooms, and the *likho* in hand, the *ved'ma* led the way through the glowing red portal. They stepped from one part of the forest to another. Here, though, the forest was all birch with yellow leaves. Among the birches, a ramshackle hut sat on stilts and was encircled by a fence made of twigs and branches. Smoke curled from the chimney, smelling of horseradish and pine. The chickens in the yard squawked and blustered away from the *likho*, even in her human shape.

"I've always found chickens to be particularly smart," said Baba Les, leading the *likho* into the hut.

With a hiss, the magical rope vanished. The *likho* rubbed her wrists where faint burn marks laced across her skin.

"For trying to curse me with bad luck," Baba Les said, gesturing to the one-room house in which they sat, "you can spend your time cleaning and organizing my house.

The *likho* grimaced.

The *ved'ma* was a packrat. She had filled her house to near-bursting with all manner of things: clay jars of every shape and size, only some labeled; herbs like chamomile, mint, dill, and horseradish; a stack of patchwork blankets and a pile of used rags; a spindle and a row of sewing needles like teeth strung on a thread; a collection of broken and unbroken chairs; an array of spoons, ladles, and knives; the bones of a fox; and much, much more.

"Don't give me that look." The *ved'ma* tapped the side of her nose knowingly. "Your tricks have killed more than a few people. You're lucky I didn't tear you to pieces."

The *likho* scowled. Could magic do that to a spirit, tear it apart? She decided she didn't want to find out. If anyone had strong enough magic, it was Baba Les. "And when I am done cleaning, you will let me go?"

Baba Les gave a short laugh. "Trees and twigs, no! When you are done, you will feed the chickens and sweep the yard and then fetch water. By the time you are done with the outside chores, the house will need cleaning again."

The *likho* felt her human heart sink deep into her belly. "It was just going to be a silly trick. Just a slippery cane or a stubbed toe. I wasn't going to give you *that* bad of luck."

The *ved'ma* shook her head. "What's done is done. You can't go around cursing people without any repercussions."

The *likho* blinked. But wasn't that exactly what she was supposed to do? She was a *likho*, a spirit of bad luck. She was meant to curse people with bad luck. It was not her fault that bad luck could mean anything from a pricked finger to an accidental pickaxe through the eye.

"You will stay here with me," said the *ved'ma*, "and that will be one less *likho* in the world."

"So … when will you let me go?" the *likho* asked.

"Do you not understand?" Baba Les said. "Never."

CHAPTER 2

Klavdiya Romanovna

Time did not pass at Baba Les's house in the same manner that it passed in the outside world; and the *likho* did her best not to count the days lest she go crazy. Instead, she performed the cleaning and the feeding each day and each night, just as Baba Les proscribed. After some time, unable to cause misfortune for the *ved'ma*, her magic began to wane. She feared that without her magic she might wink out of existence, but Baba Les assured her that spirits couldn't die – not that way, at least. That meant, of course, that the *likho* remained in servitude.

Until one day, while the *likho* was sweeping the yard, a woman appeared at Baba Les's gate.

She was perhaps thirty years of age with pale gold hair captured in a pearl-studded hairnet. She wore a copper brown *dalmatica*, the silken cuffs of her *rubakha* peeking out through the *dalmatica*'s voluminous sleeves. She flinched when she saw the *likho*. It was the singular eye, the *likho* was certain, because she otherwise had the body of any ordinary human woman. Quickly, the woman smoothed her features.

"You are not Baba Les."

The *likho* shook her head and then pointed towards the house with the broom handle.

The woman entered, crossed the yard, and then clambered into the ramshackle hut.

The *likho* cocked her head. In all the days and nights – however many they were – that she had stayed with the *ved'ma*, no one had come to visit. And this woman, in her fancy garments, seemed so certain about calling on a *ved'ma* with the power to force her into what was turning out to be eternal solitude. The *likho* turned away, continuing to sweep the chicken feces out of the yard and into the forest. Whatever business the woman had, it certainly had nothing to do with the *likho*.

Or so the *likho* thought.

Having finished the sweeping, the *likho* fetched a bag of birdseed and tossed chicken feed on the ground. Even after all this time, the chickens remained wary of her, balking until she walked away. As she put away the birdseed, the door to the hut swung open and Baba Les stuck out her head, a wisp of her iron gray hair catching in the breeze.

"*Likho*," the *ved'ma* said. "I need you inside."

The *likho* had not yet fetched the water from the stream, but she did not complain that her chores were delayed – or hopefully forgotten. Instead, she glided across the yard and up the stairs.

The inside of the house was dim; and her eye took a moment to adjust. The visitor sat at Baba Les's table, drinking a bitter-smelling brew. Again, the visitor winced when she saw the *likho*. Leaning on her cane, Baba Les hobbled to the table and sat. Then, she gestured for the *likho* to join them. The *likho* sat slowly, unused to being invited to even the smallest luxuries.

"This is Klavdiya Romanovna of Snegograd," Baba Les said. "She is fleeing an arranged marriage."

The *likho* blinked her one eye. What did the plight of a noblewoman fleeing an arranged marriage have to do with her?

"I'm in love with Boris Pavlovich." Klavdiya Romanovna clutched her cup tightly. "But my parents insist I marry the *boyar* Gavriil Gavriilovich. I cannot imagine marrying someone I don't love. I want to run away with Boris but every time I try, my parents' armsmen find me and drag me back!"

"She has come for my help," Baba Les said. "And I can give her her wish – but only if someone else will take her place. Klavdiya Romanovna offered to pay me handsomely if I would be willing to give up my one-eyed girl, rather than making her find a replacement herself."

The *likho* frowned. "I am a *likho*. I cannot marry a human."

"Baba Les, make her see reason," Klavdiya Romanovna said. "I'll cut off my own finger and give it to you, so long as you make the one-eyed girl take my place."

The *ved'ma* licked her lips as though presented with the most delectable meal. "*Likho*, I let me make two bargains today – one with Klavdiya Romanovna and one with you. If you switch places with Klavdiya Romanovna, you will have a chance to become a *likho* again. If you can convince the human man to love you, then the magic binding you to this form will break and you can return to your *likho* form and be free of me."

Be free of her. The *likho*'s palms itched. She could be rid of Baba Les and this frail body. But how did you convince a human man to love?

"Or you can stay here," Baba Les teased. "Forever."

Her magic was already fading. She could not stay here and serve Baba Les – cleaning and feeding and fetching water – for the rest of eternity. No, the *likho* would make this human man fall in love somehow. Then, she would be free. "I will do it."

"Thank Rodú," muttered Klavdiya Romanovna.

Baba Les smiled like a cat – all teeth and wide, unnatural eyes.

The *ved'ma* drew her belt knife and gestured for Klavdiya Romanovna to give her her hand. Into Klavdiya's palm, Baba Les carved a rune. Bright blood seeped through the cut, pooling in Klavdiya's palm and staining the *ved'ma*'s knife.

"No longer are you Klavdiya Romanovna of Snegograd," Baba Les said. "You are free to choose who and what you are."

"I will be Akilina Andreyevna," announced the human woman, closing her fingers around her bloody palm. "I am a free woman who is in love with Boris Pavlovich. We will be married."

Baba Les turned over the newly-named Akilina Andreyevna's hand and then sliced a second rune into the back of her hand. "Let it be done."

Magic crackled red and black, and the *likho* slunk back on her stool. Akilia Andreyevna's clothes changed. No longer did she wear a *dalmatica*, but now she wore a simple, gray *navershnik* over an even simpler, cream-colored *rubakha*. And the pearly hairnet in her hair dissolved, leaving her pale golden tresses loose around her shoulders. She looked ... younger ... than she had before.

Baba Les held out her hand. "Give me your hand, *likho*."

The *likho* laid her hand on the table, trembling slightly. In her *likho*-form, a knife would not frighten her. But her human form was weak and prone to pain. The bloody knife did not look like her friend.

"You are Klavdiya Romanovna." Baba Les dug the point of her knife into the *likho*'s palm and then dragged it through the skin there. "You are the daughter of the *boyar* of Snegograd. You are betrothed to Gavriil Gavriilovich of Makovy."

The *likho* felt the magic – crackling and burning – wrap around her. Her mind filled with strange visions of kremlins and manors that she had never seen. She smelled tallow and leather, stone and sweat. And a voice rang through her mind: *Klavdiya, Klavdiya, Klavdiya.*

Baba Les turned the *likho* – no, Klavdiya's – hand over. Swiftly, she cut another symbol into the back of Klavdiya's hand, intoning once again, "Let it be done."

Blood pooled on the tabletop in two places, dripping from both *likho*-Klavdiya's and new-Akilina's hands. Baba Les did not seem to care. Akilina started laughing, then, getting up from the table and dancing in place. Klavdiya stiffened, unsure whether she had just saved or doomed herself.

CHAPTER 3

A Broken Wheel

Likho had no need of sleep, and so they didn't. However, the *likho* named Klavdiya woke up on a padded bench in a carriage – which meant she had slept. She scowled. Even at Baba Les's house, she did not sleep. She rubbed her temples. She did not remember leaving the *ved'ma*'s house. She held up her hand, where the runes the *ved'ma* had carved were now faint scars. The witch had sent her here … somehow.

"Klava, dear." A woman with gray in her dark brown hair sat across from Klavdiya, and she was drawing back the curtain. She wore a black *dalmatica* over a coal-gray *rubakha* as well as layers of silver jewelry. She smelled distinctly of beef tallow. Klavdiya guessed she was a noblewoman. "Look."

Klavdiya glanced through the foggy window. Beyond the glass were fields struggling to produce barley and an old, wooden manor with a red-tiled roof.

"That is the Makovy estate," the noblewoman said.

You are betrothed to Gavriil Gavriilovich of Makovy.

Klavdiya flinched, remembering her bargain with the *ved'ma*. She would take the real Klavdiya's place. The antiquated house belonged to a man who she would marry. Who she had to convince to love her. Her stomach twisted. Surely, this situation was better than being trapped in servitude to Baba Les for all eternity. Still, she did not want to marry and seduce a human man.

I am a likho. *I cannot marry a human.*

And can they love me?

"Do not scowl so, Klava," said the noblewoman. "You will

give yourself wrinkles. Lord Gavriil Gavriilovich is expecting a young, unwrinkled wife!"

Klavdiya rubbed her forehead. Could scowling *actually* give humans wrinkles?

"And please, stop with your silent treatment," the noblewoman scolded. "No one wants to marry a woman who refuses to talk."

So, the original Klavdiya – now Akilina – had been refusing to speak in protest of her marriage. This "silent treatment" as the noblewoman called it served Klavdiya. She didn't know what relation she was meant to have with this other woman. Nor did she know how many mistakes she could make before the woman realized that Klavdiya wasn't *actually* Klavdiya. Or not the Klavdiya this woman knew.

She ran her fingers over the scars on her hand and said nothing.

The noblewoman sighed loudly and pinched the bridge of her nose. "Fine. You do not need to speak to your own mother, but I beg you to speak to your new husband."

This woman was the original Klavdiya's mother, but she could not tell that her own daughter had disappeared and a *likho* had taken her place? Klavdiya wondered if all humans were this easily tricked. Maybe it would be easy to seduce the man Gavriil Gavriilovich.

Her hope caused her magic – long suppressed by Baba Les – to crackle around her. Though staring directly at Klavdiya, the noblewoman seemed not to notice. Klavdiya tried to pull her magic closer, but it slipped through her grasp.

A loud pop sounded outside, and the carriage came to a sharp stop.

Someone rapped on the window. "My lady, a wheel has broken."

Klavdiya fumbled with the latch and then swung open the door. She stumbled over the step attached to the carriage and onto the muddy road. The wind twisted her hair and pulled at her clothes – the same copper-colored *dalmatica* the original Klavdiya had been wearing. The footman and driver looked at her in surprise, but again they did not seem to realize that she *wasn't* the real Klavdiya. Grabbing fistfuls of her skirts, she took several strides towards the manor house. She had a *boyar* to seduce and her freedom to win.

"Klava, Klava!" The noblewoman leaned out of the carriage. "You cannot just walk to the Makovy manor. You will be covered in mud."

Klavdiya kept walking, her gaze locked on the manor. What did a little mud matter? The footman hurried after her, trying to bar her way. She closed her hands into fists. He was in her way. Her magic hissed around her, and the footman slipped and fell on his backside. She stepped around him.

She strode down the road, even as a faint drizzle started.

Halfway to the manor, she was met by two men on horseback. The first was a dark-haired man draped in a fine wool coat with cornflowers embroidered at the shoulders. Just behind him rode a blond, mustached man in a padded leather vest.

The first man's gaze swept across her and then honed in on the details, hesitating on her single eye. Or perhaps the lack of the second one. "My lady Klavdiya Romanovna?"

She stood still for a long moment, looking up at his narrow face and sky-blue eyes. Then, she remembered her new name. Shaking herself minutely, she nodded.

He swung from his saddle and then bowed his head. "I am Gavriil Gavriilovich. It is my honor to make your acquaintance."

So this was the man who she would marry, who she would convince to love her so that she could escape Baba Les. She held herself straighter. "The carriage. Its wheel. It broke."

"Mikhail, ride ahead," Gavriil said to his blond companion. "Make sure that Lady Antonina Antonovna and her people are well. I will take the lady Klavdiya Romanovna back to the manor and send the wheelwright."

The man named Mikhail opened his mouth as though to protest, but then he shut it, nodded, and urged his horse on.

In one smooth motion, Gavriil dismounted. Unclasping his

embroidered cloak, he offered it to Klavdiya. As she settled it on her shoulders, she inhaled the fresh scent of rosemary and her skin prickled. Gavriil laced his hands and kneeled, his palms facing upward on his knee. "Allow me to help you mount."

Klavdiya looked at the horse skeptically. When she moved towards it, it shied away from her. Gavriil caught the reins and spoke quietly to the beast. The whites of its eyes still showed, but it allowed her to approach. For a moment, Klavdiya wondered if her "betrothed" might be magicked somehow – to be able to calm a horse spooked by a *likho* – but she sensed no magic in Gavriil. The horse simply ... trusted ... him. Gavriil gave her a leg up, and then she sat upon the beast's back. It shivered beneath her once, but it permitted her to ride it.

Gavriil took the reins, turning the horse towards the manor. "I did not expect to meet my bride on the road, my lady."

A *likho* was used to her own company. And when Klavdiya served Baba Les, she did not speak to the *ved'ma*. But she guessed that humans – chatty creatures that they were – did not fall in love unless they were spoken to. She didn't know what to say, though, so she settled on mirroring his words. "I did not expect to meet you either."

He bowed his head. "Forgive me, I did not mean offense. I simply meant that you are intrepid, walking ahead of your carriage in the rain."

"Do you dislike intrepid?" She would make certain to be less bold, less intrepid.

"Not at all," he assured her. "It is simply uncommon amongst noblewomen."

"And you wish to have a common bride?"

Gavriil laughed, and she felt something strange inside her belly. "Intrepid and clever."

Klavdiya tilted her head and narrowed her eyes. She could not tell if he liked how she acted or not. How was she supposed to seduce him if she could not read him? She should have realized how hard this bargain would be. A *likho* didn't care about human emotions beyond bringing misfortune and misery. She didn't know what *love* might look like.

He sobered when he saw her expression. “My lady, I promise that you will be cherished in Makovy.”

She gripped the pommel of the saddle. She didn’t need to be cherished. She needed to be loved so that she could escape this marriage and this human body, so she could be a *likho* again.

CHAPTER 4

Threads Entwine

Likho did not marry. They much preferred a solitary life and solitary hunting. Lugging around a *likho*-spouse would either cause too much bad luck or require the two *likho* to share one victim. In the case of the former, *likho* were scrupulous in allotting bad luck; it was human action or inaction that caused a small bit of bad luck to balloon. In the case of the latter, no *likho* would want to share their prey.

So Klavdiya found herself stumbling through every aspect of human marriage – so much so that she feared that someone might notice something was off.

First, there was the dress. From Antonina Antonovna's and the maids' reactions, the red-brown *rubakha* and the wine-red *navershnik* embroidered with tan quails layered on top were special. Klavdiya could not tell what was different about them than what she had worn before.

"Gavriil Gavriilovich won't be able to take his eyes off you," Antonina said as the maid pinned temple rings to Klavdiya's headband.

Klavdiya picked at the clasp on her heavy, silver bracelet. From her short time alone with Gavriil Gavriilovich, she had determined that he was particularly interested in her lack of an eye. "I expect him to look at my eye, not my clothes."

Antonina sighed, shaking her head minutely. "You are the daughter of a *boyar*. He will forget about your missing eye soon enough."

Hopefully very quickly. Klavdiya did not want to be stuck in this farce of a marriage for any longer than she had to. The quicker Gavriil Gavriilovich forgot about her singular eye, the quicker he would fall in love with her. She would also have to determine whether he *liked* an intrepid and clever bride, or if she needed to pretend to be meek and slow to earn his love. Again, none of that had anything to do with her clothes.

When Antonina Antonovna was satisfied with Klavdiya's attire, Klavdiya was ushered out of her private room. In the main hall, a bald nun in a white habit awaited them. Klavdiya hung back. *Likho* and nuns were not friends. On more than a few occasions, a nun had exorcised Klavdiya, leaving her confused and in pain for days afterwards. This time though, the nun simply fell alongside Antonina Antonovna as they left the main hall, passed through the foyer, and then exited the manor house. Klavdiya, Antonina, the nun, and two maids walked through the courtyard and then down a sloping hillside. They passed through a lacquered garden gate and then through a garden carpeted with tiny snowdrops and edged with blooming crocus. At the end of the garden path, a pair of willow trees sheltered a pond with water that was still and silver like a mirror.

In dark trousers and a ruby-red caftan, Gavriil Gavriilovich waited at the pondside along with a string of noblemen, including the blond-haired Mikhail who had met Klavdiya on the road the other day, and manservants. Gavriil stepped forward, offering his hand to Klavdiya.

She took his hand stiffly. When did *likho* hold hands? They wrapped their limbs around their victims' necks and held on tightly.

"You look lovely today, my lady," Gavriil said, even as his gaze flickered to her missing eye.

She was certain he was lying, but she kept her mouth shut. She inclined her head.

"Sister Inna." Gavriil turned to the nun. "If you would marry us?"

"It would be my honor, my lord." The nun curtsied.

The nun drew a rough, red yarn from her pocket. She lifted

the yarn towards the sky. Mikhail stepped forward and cut the yarn in two with his belt knife. Then, the nun fastened one half of the cord around Gavriil's throat. When she turned to Klavdiya, Klavdiya flinched, but the yarn did not hurt. This was no exorcism – and no one expected her. Biting the inside of her cheek, she allowed the nun to secure the yarn with a knot.

"These cords symbolize," the nun explained, "how we are all made of the same cord, twisted into existence by Rodú." She gestured. "Now, I will read the couple's fortune."

Two manservants hurried forward, one with a mirror and one with a brown egg. The first held the mirror horizontal while the nun took the egg, spoke more words, and then cracked it onto the mirror's surface. The nun inspected the egg and mirror gravely before speaking.

"Threads entwine, yet misfortune cling to the weave," said the nun. "To know the design of fate, one must first step beyond its pattern."

Klavdiya stiffened. Of course, misfortune clung to the threads of fate. That misfortune was her. Gavriil squeezed her hand and offered an encouraging smile.

The manservants carried away the sullied mirror, and Antonina led the maids in bringing forward white purses stitched with roses. Inside the purses were rings and coins – all silver – which were poured into Klavdiya's and Gavriil's hands. Klavdiya had no idea what to do, so she mimicked Gavriil. He stepped to the very edge of the water and then tossed his handfuls of rings and coins into the water. Klavdiya did the same and watched as a *vodnik* appeared, its froglike eyes blinking at her as though to ask, *Why is a* likho *pretending to get married?*

"May the spirits of the water accept our gift," the nun said, "and bless this marriage."

Klavdiya frowned as the *vodnik* reached out its webbed claws, collecting. Why did the water spirits get offerings during human marriage? *Likho* never got offerings.

After a moment, she realized that everyone was looking at her. Her face felt hot. What had she missed? Would they realize that she was not human, that she was not the *real* Klavdiya?

Gavriil reached for her hand again. “Are you ready, my lady?”

Klavdiya’s magic crackled around her; she did not know why. She only knew that she must take Gavriil’s hand and say “Yes.”

Gavriil guided her into the chilly water until they were calf-deep. Her skirts floated around her legs like spilled blood. Gavriil stepped close enough that she could smell his rosemary scent. He placed a hand on her lower back, making her feel strange, his other hand tightening around hers. Then, he leaned her back and dunked her into the water.

She came up spluttering and angry. Her magic hissed, lashing out in black tendrils. The mirror in the manservant’s hands broke with a loud *pop*, shedding millions of crystalline pieces onto the ground. The man’s left hand was bloody.

Gavriil guided Klavdiya from the water. “Get Pyotr back to the house,” he told the nearest servant. “Margarita can bandage him up.”

The nun was pale. She held up a finger. “My lord–”

“It is done,” Gavriil said. “The lady Klavdiya Romanovna and I are married. There’s nothing else to discuss.”

While Antonina Antonovna looked pleased, the rest of the party wore a variety of grimaces and scowls. Klavdiya drew her hand away from Gavriil, taking in each expression. Did a bad fortune and a broken mirror spell doom? Then, she turned to Gavriil. He didn’t look bothered. And that was all that mattered: that he could still fall in love with her.

CHAPTER 5

Cursed

Staring through the sitting room window out onto the garden, Gavriil twisted the red yarn at his throat. A future to which misfortune clung didn't surprise him. Rodú, the god of fate, was not kind to Gavriil. But the broken mirror – that was a sign that the god did not approve of this marriage. A grave sign. But Gavriil *needed* Klavdiya. Rather, he needed access to her father's lands, the right to hunt on Snegograd lands. No matter what Rodú thought, Gavriil would remain married to Klavdiya at least until he got hunting rights.

Unfortunately, Mikhail Petrovich and Sister Inna did not share his pragmatic view of the situation. Mikhail Petrovich sat beside him on the settee, his arms crossed and an ankle resting on the opposite knee. Sister Inna sat across from them, rubbing her bare scalp with both hands.

"You cannot ignore a sign from Rodú," Sister Inna said, shaking her head. "I have *never* seen Rodú break a mirror. This marriage is ill-fated. I would worry about disasters and tragedies."

"It's my only hope for a miracle," Gavriil said, running his fingers along the yarn. It was another omen: the longer the yarn remained tied and in place, the longer and happier the marriage would be. So far, Gavriil's yarn had not fallen off. It was the best sign he had.

"Clearly, you won't get your miracle." The nun stood and began pacing "Rodú has cursed your marriage."

"You should have sent the Snegograd women back the moment you saw Klavdiya Romanovna," Mikhail Petrovich said, gesturing grandiosely. "They sent a girl with one eye? That's a clear insult and trick."

"She is the *boyar*'s daughter," Gavriil said diplomatically. "What does it matter if she has one eye or three? I didn't have any stipulations about my bride, only that I would have access to hunt Snegograd's lands."

Klavdiya's missing eye was ... interesting. Most nobility, presented with a child with such a blemish, would have deemed their daughter unmarriageable and sent her to a convent. Perhaps Lord Roman and Lady Antonina of Snegograd loved their daughter too much to send her away; and perhaps they could sense Gavriil's desperation in seeking an alliance with Snegograd. A marriage to a *boyar* was certainly better than Klavdiya or her parents had reason to expect.

"They have embarrassed you." Mikhail pounded a fist against his thigh. "Not to mention that they've incurred Rodú's wrath and put us in its path."

"Be careful what you say about Klavdiya Romanovna," Gavriil warned. "She is my wife and the Lady of Makovy. I expect her – and her family – to be treated with respect"

Mikhail's nostrils flared as he sighed, leaning his head forward. "Gavrik, do you have to be so stubborn?"

"I'm dying, Misha." He met Mikhail's gaze and held it, regardless of the pain that both of them carried. "I can either be stubborn or give up. I choose to be stubborn."

"Such an ill-fated marriage cannot be good for you," Sister Inna said, her pacing slowing. "Stubborn or no, I wouldn't wish to offend a god."

"My last hope is the firebird feather," Gavriil said. "And Snegograd is one of the few places where firebirds are known to nest. I cannot repudiate Klavdiya Romanovna, not now. Not when I still need access to her father's lands and the firebirds therein."

"I will pray and scry for another way, my lord." Sister Inna curtsied. "I will take my leave and go to the convent. Perhaps the other nuns can help as well."

Gavriil dismissed her.

"You could have just paid Snegograd," muttered Mikhail, rubbing the stubble on his chin.

Gavriil *tsk*ed and shook his head. "You know that Lord Roman is an isolationist. He hasn't had an alliance or gone to court at Rodgorod since taking the *boyar*ship from his father twenty-five years ago. I am lucky that he had a daughter to marry at all; otherwise I would have no hope of accessing his lands or his firebirds."

"You deserve better than..." Mikhail trailed off and shook his head. "You deserve a beautiful wife and a loving marriage."

"I *need* a firebird feather and we'll hope it cures me." Gavriil couldn't consider beauty or love, not when he was dying. He clapped his friend on the shoulder. "So long as my and Klavdiya's marriage is peaceful and I can get a firebird feather from it, then I will be happy."

"What if the nun is right?" Mikhail said. "What if your marriage is cursed?"

Gavriil twisted the yarn at his throat again. Would their marriage truly be so disastrous that they would want to end it? The omens at their wedding certainly seemed to think so. "I wonder if our marriage is truly doomed, or if it is my own bad luck that the omens portend – and it has nothing to do with Klavdiya Romanovna."

"I pray not," said Mikhail. "I have known you since you fostered at my father's house, and I plan to know you well into old age."

Gavriil squeezed his friend's shoulder. "To old age."

"To old age, Gavrik."

CHAPTER 6

Snowdrops and Crocus

Gavriil found Klavdiya alone in the solar. She wore a dark ensemble and huddled in the darkest corner with an embroidery hoop in hand. She appeared to be almost a shadow at first glance. As he came closer, he saw that she had done little more than thread the needle and make the first stitch. She held the needle as though ready to continue but remained still – as though only miming the movements.

He straightened his silver-trimmed caftan and then ran a hand through his dark hair before asking, "No inspiration, my lady?"

She started and stabbed the needle into the canvas. She must have struck herself because a bloody splotch bloomed on the fabric.

A small pang of guilt striking him, he pulled the kerchief from his pocket. "Forgive me, my lady, I did not mean to startle you."

Klavdiya said nothing as Gavriil sat slowly in the upholstered chair beside her. He had noticed, over the past few days, that she was prone to silences. He did not think she meant them as an insult but was rather preoccupied with her own thoughts. He had tried a few times to guess what she might be thinking of, but he could come up with nothing beyond post-marital nerves.

"I have been busy these past few days," he began, making sure to look at her good eye and not the missing one that hid behind a silken, black eyepatch. "I have been so busy handling the post-nuptial celebrations that I have scarcely had time to speak to you." She still remained silent, though she met his gaze. "I do not mean to neglect you, my lady."

"You have been busy," she echoed, wrapping his kerchief around her wounded finger. "I ... do not fault you."

He reached out to touch her hand, and she flinched. He bit the inside of his cheek. Was she nervous? He could not imagine that the intrepid and clever woman he met on the road was truly nervous. Instead, he feared that she did not like her husband. In the same way that most men would find her missing eye repulsive, she found something about Gavriil ... lacking.

He told himself that thought was ridiculous. He didn't need a wife who liked him.

Klavdiya slowly drew the needle through the hoop, adding a second yellow stitch to the now-stained fabric. "Are you happy with your marriage?"

"Of course," Gavriil said. He could not let Klavdiya or anyone else hear otherwise. He needed access to Snegograd's lands and to the firebirds that nested there. He would not fail in finding a firebird feather – the cure to his illness – because of stupid things like his advisors' superstition or some misplaced desire for love within a political marriage. "Though it has been a short marriage, it has been smooth and pleasant."

She gripped the embroidery hoop and stared down at its mostly-blank canvas. His ears burned. She, clearly, was not as happy as he pretended to be.

"I'm certain it's difficult being away from everything and everyone you know," he said. "If I can help ease that transition, please let me know."

Klavdiya looked up. "You are turning red."

Gavriil let out a wheezing laugh. This woman was bold. He lied again, "It's a bit warm."

She inclined her head towards the window. "It is cooler outside."

Oh, she was suggesting they take a walk. Did she find the solar stuffy? Gavriil decided – for the time being – that he would not ask. He had his whole life to learn about his new wife's likes and dislikes. He rushed to his feet and proffered his arm. "Join me, my lady."

She raised her eyebrows and studied his arm as though she had never been offered a man's arm before. Then, she set down her embroidery and settled her hand upon his forearm, letting him guide her to her feet. A few corridors and one staircase later, they stepped out into the brisk spring air and passed through the garden gate. Makovy's *boyars* and *boyarynyas* grew cornflowers, the symbol of their house. However, it was not yet cornflower's season, so instead the gardener had planted snowflowers and crocus. The old, weeping willows shaded the space, their long vines just beginning to sprout little, green buds.

"A *vodnik* lives in your pond," said Klavdiya, drawing away from him and walking to the silvery pond that glowed silver in the corner of the garden. She peered at the water as though expecting the creature to emerge at any moment.

"I've never seen any *vodyanoy*." Gavriil followed her to the pondside. "And no one has drowned here."

"It is because you feed it silver."

He smiled. "We only do that for marriages, my lady."

"You must have plenty of marriages," she said.

"We're a large estate," he replied. "There are enough marriages. Though enough to placate a vengeful spirit?"

"You gave it enough silver to last it a year or more at your– my– *our* wedding."

Gavriil bent down and plucked a crocus. Stepping closer to his wife, he offered it to her. "You know plenty about the desires of spirits. Are there many in Snegograd?"

Klavdiya slowly twirled the crocus between her thumb and forefinger, tilting her head to the side. She did not answer, and so his follow-up question – about Snegograd's firebirds – remained silent. She turned away from the pond, her coal-gray skirts sashaying silently across the gravel path. If he did not know better, he might have thought her a shadow. The idea made him want to reach out and grasp her, to prove that shadows could be held. He shook his head. That was absurd. She was as much a woman as he was a man. Real in all senses of the word.

And he shouldn't want to grasp her, hold her. He was using her. He did not deserve her affections.

"You know," he said, "the garden is my favorite place on the estate."

She paused, looking at him over her shoulder.

"It reminds me of Lukyomorya, the magical land in poetry," he said.

"You like poetry?" she said.

"Do you like it?" His pulse quickened. Perhaps they would have poetry in common, something to talk about so that their encounters were not so awkward.

She moved away from him again to drag her fingers along the willow's trunk. "I will listen to a *skazka* or *bylina* on occasion."

"I've always preferred love poetry," he said. "But I know a *bylina* or two.

"In Lukomorya, there's wonder abound:
The leshy *lives in his forest surround;*
A blue-eyed rusalka *carols and sings;*
And the ruby-scaled zmey *takes his wing."*

Klavdiya smiled softly. Gavriil swallowed against a sudden tightness in his throat. She was like a wilted flower – beautiful in a tragic way. Her ink-black braid cascaded down her back, threaded with ribbon; and her layers of black and gray fluttered around her like flower petals, tempting him to touch her and find out where her clothes ended and her body began. Did he find his one-eyed wife *beautiful*? Truly? He told himself that it wasn't possible, that she was a tool and no man found his hammer beautiful.

His illness catching up with him, he found a bench and sat, watching her. If he found Klavdiya lovely – even in an esoteric way – it would make his marital duties easier.

She came to him then, holding a cluster of tiny snowdrops in her hand. She proffered the bouquet to him.

He laughed, taking them from her.

"Why do you laugh at me?" she asked.

"I laugh from joy," he said. "It is a man's duty to give flowers to his woman. It is a gift when a woman gives them to her man."

She narrowed her eye, even as she sat beside him. She opened her mouth as though to contradict him but then faltered. She raised her hand and hesitated, leaving it hanging in the air. "Your nose. It's bleeding."

Gavriil touched his face and cursed. Sure enough, his nose bled. He had given Klavdiya his kerchief and now it was nowhere to be found, so he wiped his nose with the sleeve of his caftan. "Forgive me, my lady."

"I-I'm sorry," she murmured, her hand falling to his shoulder.

"It's nothing." He shook his head, dabbing off the rest of the blood.

She blinked. "It's bad luck."

He nodded, putting his hand over hers. "It happens sometimes."

She muttered, barely audible, "It happens sometimes..."

CHAPTER 7

The One-Eyed Bride

Klavdiya belonged not to sweet words and flowers, but to shadows and the coldest hours of the night. But when she thought of Gavriil's voice, deep and clear as he recited lines from the *bylina*, she felt a strange pang in her chest. When she thought about him saying, about bad luck, *it happens sometimes*, that pang grew larger and more painful. She did not know why because, certainly, a *likho* couldn't feel desire – not like this. Desire for a victim, desire to cause misfortune – yes. Desire for a human man – laughable.

A knock sounded at the door and Klavdiya's lady's maid opened it. The steward – a short and thin man with glassy blue eyes – bowed deeply, his hands shaking. Klavdiya wasn't certain if something was wrong or if he simply found Klavdiya unsettling like most of the servants did.

"Lord Gavriil Gavriilovich requests your company, my lady," he said.

Klavdiya stood and gestured for the steward to lead. She needed no more fussing from Elvira. The steward turned several shades paler, but he guided her down the corridor and to a small sitting room with two upholstered settees and a single sidet able with an unlit candle.

Gavriil sat in the dark room, his only light coming from the single curtain-less window. He stood slowly, turning to face her. He wore snugly-fitted trousers, polished boots, and a pleated tunic. No silk-trimmed caftan or silver jewelry this time. Klavdiya was not sure why she noticed his clothes. That seemed a very human thing to do. She hoped that she was not becoming more human with each passing day. If so, she needed to figure out how to seduce Gavriil so that she could return to her *likho* form.

"My lady," he said, gesturing to a chair opposite from him. "Please, sit."

Klavdiya took her seat carefully, watching him. "You look tired."

His fingers tightened on the chair's arms for a moment. Then, he eased back into the chair. "I have had trouble sleeping these past days."

"Why?" She cocked her head. She wondered if it was her presence. Perhaps she was causing him nightmares or aches and pains during the night. Their rooms shared a wall. She was certainly close enough to cause him misfortune.

"I wanted to speak to you about something." A piece of his dark hair fell onto his forehead and brushed against his eyebrow.

Not about his sleep? She squinted. She did not quite understand how humans could flit from one conversation topic to the other. When she did not wish to speak about something, she simply remained silent.

"My lady, I do not know how swiftly word travels," he began, "but if you did not know, I am ill."

"Ill?" she echoed, leaning forward. "Ill how?"

"It is a miasma of the blood," Gavriil said. "I have had it for two years now. It's slowly draining me. It makes me fatigued, mostly. But bruise easily and get sick more often than I should."

Her human heart beat harder. "Are you dying?"

"If I don't find the cure."

Her nails dug into the fine upholstery of the settee on which she sat. Gavriil could not die. If he did, she would be stuck as a human. No, he had to live long enough to fall in love with her. "What is the cure?"

"I have tried everything from Rodú's knotted threads to physician's tinctures to a *ved'ma*'s runes," he said. "My last hope is a firebird's feather, crushed and mixed with cumin and rhubarb."

"A firebird's feather?" Klavdiya could barely fathom the task at hand. Being an exceedingly rare creature, firebirds were also suspicious and flighty. It would be a miracle for Gavriil to *find* a firebird; it would be a second miracle for him to catch one and take its feather.

"I know they live on your father's estate," said Gavriil. "So I am asking that you write to your father and beg his permission to allow me to hunt firebirds on his lands."

My father? She frowned. *Oh.* Yes, the real Klavdiya had a father, just like she had a mother Antonina Antonovna. *Likho*-Klavdiya tended to forget that because *likho* did not have parents. They simply existed.

"Write it for me," Klavdiya said. "I do not know how to write."

Gavriil's gaze flickered across her face, his expression enigmatic. Then, he said, "Of course, my lady, I would be happy to."

He rang a bell on the side table and requested that a servant bring in birchbark paper, ink, and a quill. When the writing implements arrived, he served as Klavdiya's scribe, writing the quick and simple request she sent to her "father" asking for hunting rights. Gavriil, then, penned his own and pressed it with a wax seal.

Klavdiya reached across the distance separating them. Her hand clasped atop his knee. "Do not die."

He let out a small laugh. "I am trying not to."

"You always laugh at me." She peered up at him. "I am not being funny."

"I am laughing at my own desperation," he replied, settling his hand upon hers. His fingers were warm. "No one wants to die, my lady. Me, least of all. I have a whole *boyar*dom and a new wife that I want to live for."

"Certainly, you do not want to live for me." She knew how he looked at her eye and her gray pallor. He wasn't enamored with her. "You do not even know me."

"If I die, I will never have the chance to know you." He squeezed her hand, and her pulse quickened strangely. "I might not have expected my one-eyed bride, but she is bold and witty and has a unique perspective. She is worth knowing, is she not?"

Klavdiya felt hot. It was such a strange sensation. She never remembered being hot before. She was always cold. A *likho* was always cold. Her magic hissed and wriggled around her. The unlit candle toppled over onto its side. Neither she nor Gavriil paid it any heed.

"Yes," she said because she needed him to know her – or a version of her that he could fall in love with.

CHAPTER 8

A Firebird's Trail

"I think the lady is enamored with you," Mikhail Petrovich said, following behind Gavriil on horseback as they took a leisurely ride. The sun peeked from between heavy, blue-gray clouds that threatened spring rain; and the grass track that circled the manor glimmered with dew.

"She is eager to please." Gavriil inhaled the smell of petrichor and crocus, remembering the sight of Klavdiya in the garden. How she was as beautiful as a shadow, her skirts multilayered and dark like a nighttime blossom. He had wanted to touch her, then.

"If she didn't look so dour, I might compare her to a puppy," said Mikhail, "keeping to your side with such eager devotion."

"She is worried about me."

"*I* am worried about you," his friend said, urging his black horse to walk quicker in order to ride side-by-side with Gavriil. "I don't put much faith in omens, but a broken mirror on your wedding day is as clear *and bad* of an omen as there is. And I have told you about my misgivings about the Lord of Snegograd's honesty."

Gavriil repressed a sigh as they turned the final corner of their ride. From here, the grass track ran straight back to the manor's front courtyard. He did not want Mikhail to worry about him. He did not want his new bride to worry about him. He didn't want anyone to worry about him. He would much rather be healthy and hale than searching desperately for a cure to this slow death.

"And I have impressed upon you the importance of this

marriage." He touched the red yarn that remained around his throat. The longer it remained on his neck, the better it boded. "I'm not in a place to turn away my bride."

Mikhail was quiet for a long moment, his blue gaze icy as he squinted at the path before him. Then, he said, "Have you consummated the marriage?"

Gavriil bristled. "That is a bold question."

Mikhail sighed, his shoulders sagging. "Of course, you haven't. It's for the best, Gavrik. Keep her at arm's length. Then, if there is any foul play or foul luck, you can still annul the marriage."

"I have no plans of annulling the marriage," said Gavriil firmly as they approached the manor. "But I want Klavdiya Romanovna to have the option to have the marriage voided, should I die. Her father and mother have clearly protected her this long. She will be safe in their care, if I am gone; and they can find her another suitable husband."

"Gavrik, you know no one else will..." Mikhail sighed again, louder this time. "May she be as lucky in her second marriage as she is in this one."

"Hopefully, there won't be a second marriage." Gavriil dismounted and led his palomino horse into the courtyard. The sound of iron horse shoes on stone rang through the air.

"May Rodú be merciful" – Mikhail swung out of his own saddle – "and let you live a long and healthy life."

Already, Rodú had dictated that Gavriil would live a sickly life – but Gavriil didn't say that. There was still a chance that he might find the firebird feather and that the feather might cure his blood miasma.

Passing the horses to a stableboy, the two men entered the manor. The foyer was lit by the multi-colored light straining through the stained glass windows that decorated the manor's façade with images of *zmey* and *leshy* and *bolotniki*. A long woven rug in red, green, and white stretched from the front door to the end of the foyer, which opened into the main hall.

Klavdiya Romanovna stood to the side of the hall's doorway,

a piece of birchbark paper in her pale hands. In the corner, as she was, she looked ... otherworldly. Her black *dalmatica* blended into the shadows; and, braided around her head, her hair looked like an inky black crown. Her skin, too, seemed almost silvery as though she were made from mist and not flesh. She took a step forward.

"My lady." Gavriil opened his hand in greeting.

"A letter came from Snegograd." She held out the birchbark paper. "Will you read it?"

Feeling Mikhail's gaze on the back of his head, Gavriil took the missive. He was surprised that a beloved daughter like Klavdiya did not know how to read or write, but not every Ruthenian lord saw fit to teach his daughters in the same manner he might teach a son. Gavriil smoothed the paper with his thumb, staring down at the angular script hatching across the birchbark.

A slow smile crept onto his face. "Lord Roman Avdeyevich has agreed to allow us to hunt for a firebird on his lands."

Klavdiya clutched her chest, her head lowered; and Mikhail clasped Gavriil on the shoulder.

"Thank you, my lady," Gavriil said after a moment, "for writing to your father."

"I will accompany you," Klavdiya blurted.

"Of course," Gavriil said.

Gavriil sensed Mikhail stiffening behind him. But what did it matter that Klavdiya wished to return to Snegograd? Whether she wanted to help Gavriil find his cure or she wanted to see her home, neither motive seemed troublesome. And Gavriil planned on bringing a retinue to Snegograd anyway; one more person would not significantly burden him.

"You can show me around Snegograd, my lady," Gavriil said.

Klavdiya faltered but then nodded earnestly, "Yes, and I will help you find your firebird."

He raised an eyebrow. "Do you know where they nest, my lady?"

She shook her head. "I will find them."

Gavriil hesitated. She was so certain. But how? Firebirds were incredibly elusive and rare creatures. "Have you seen them before?"

"Three times," she said. "But they leave a distinctive ... trail."

"Traveling the wilderness will be a significant hardship for her ladyship," protested Mikhail. "Perhaps you will tell Lord Gavriil and I what this 'trail' looks like. Then you can remain comfortably in Snegograd while the hunters find the firebird."

Her expression grew hard. "You cannot see it."

Mikhail snorted. "I can certainly see better than you."

"Mikhail Petrovich," Gavriil growled in warning.

At least his friend had the grace to bow his head and mutter an apology. Klavdiya folded her arms and did not look impressed. Gavriil bit the inside of his cheek, his fingers crunching through the birchbark letter. He could not have his closest friend and his wife at odds.

"You do not *see* the firebird's trail," Klavdiya said. "Not unless you know how."

That made Mikhail even tenser. Gavriil quickly asked, "What do you mean, my lady?"

"The firebird is magic," she said. "You have to see magic."

The hairs on the back of Gavriil's neck stood on end. "And you can see it? Magic, I mean?"

She nodded, her expression utterly serious.

Gavriil took a deep breath. "Are you a *ved'ma*?"

Klavdiya met his gaze. Her eyes held fear and another emotion akin to a desperate, grasping need.

CHAPTER 9

Red for Peonies

Determining what Gavriil desired in a wife was turning out to be impossible. He told her that she was intrepid and clever. He laughed when she meant to be serious. He told her he would cherish and protect her, whether she was a *ved'ma* or not, even though Klavdiya insisted that she was *not* a *ved'ma*. Gavriil was so … so … amicable. He seemed to have no preference at all.

Which made wooing him unachievable.

She sat on her bed with a harrumph, propping her elbow on her knee and her chin on her fist. She was never going to find a way to make him love her.

Across the bedchamber, Klavdiya's lady's maid, Elvira, folded clothes and set them into a traveling trunk emblazoned with a red peony on a white background. While it was difficult for Klavdiya to tell ages, she guessed that Elvira was young because her hair was so dark that it almost seemed purple with not a hint of gray or lightening. The girl also had almost eerily smooth skin. Klavdiya might have thought her a *vila* or something else enchanted if she wasn't so, well, unmagical.

"Does everyone in Snegograd dress so dourly?" Elvira asked, holding up one of Klavdiya's coal-gray *rubakha* – this one embroidered with silver lilies around the sleeves and collar.

Klavdiya didn't know. She had never been to Snegograd. "I like black."

"I have gathered that, my lady." Elvira folded the dress and placed it into the traveling trunk along with the other items headed for Snegograd.

"You are required to wear red," Klavdiya said, straightening. "For Makovy, which means peony."

"Aren't Snegograd's colors white and gold?" Elvira pulled another black item from the wardrobe. "I am surprised you like black so much." Then, the lady's maid smirked. "Perhaps you were sick of looking at such bright colors. I certainly can get tired of wearing red all the time."

Klavdiya went to the wardrobe, pulling out a black *dalmatica* with white stitching at the collar. "Take this. Wear black. You are my maid."

Elvira raised her brows, her eyes wide. Then, she dipped into a curtsy, clutching the dalmatica to her chest almost hungrily. "Thank you, my lady, thank you."

Klavdiya sensed she could twist the conversation and the young woman's gratitude to her own needs. She needed a way to woo Gavriil, and maybe a color might do it. "Does Gavriil like red? Would he like to see me wear red?"

The maid paused, considered, and then nodded. "He might like to see you in his house's colors."

Nodding, Klavdiya asked, "Where do I find red clothes?"

"I will call for the weaver and the seamstress," Elvira said, setting aside the *dalmatica* and continuing to pack Klavdiya's clothes for the trip to Snegograd. "You can pick the fabric and have dresses made to fit you. Lord Gavriil will appreciate your thoughtfulness."

Klavdiya nodded again and then drifted away, but she must have worn her thoughts upon her face because the maid asked:

"My lady, what is it?"

The bed ropes squeaked as Klavdiya sat on the bed. She considered whether to ask the question she had been thinking since making the bargain with Baba Les. She worried that it might sound foolish to a human, that a human would know the answer instantly. Only *likho* and other spirits would be at such a loss. Would Elvira think her ridiculous? Or would the girl be suspicious if Klavdiya asked such a question? She searched the maid's face. The girl seemed earnest enough; and she had been helpful from the moment Gavriil had assigned her to Klavdiya.

"How do you make a man love you?" Klavdiya asked.

"Oh, my lady," Elvira said softly. She took a step closer, her skirt quietly swishing against the stone floor. "Is that what you have been worrying about?"

"Yes," Klavdiya said. What else would she be worried about except being stuck as a human for all eternity? If Gavriil fell in love with her, she could finally be free.

"You can't *make* anyone fall in love with you," Elvira said. "You can only be yourself and hope that is enough."

Klavdiya blinked at the girl. Klavdiya was a *likho*. A spirit of bad luck. *Herself* wasn't something that someone could love. "What if it isn't enough? There must be something else?"

Elvira came closer slowly as though approaching a bird with a broken wing. "My lady, is everything all right with Lord Gavriil?"

"It is fine," Klavdiya snapped and then said, softer, "It is too *fine*."

"You want more passion?"

"I want him to love me."

"Does he treat you well? Is he kind? Does he respect you?" Elvira said. "That is more than most of us have. Rodú blessed your marriage – I don't care what the omens said. If his lordship treats you well, then you are very, very lucky."

Klavdiya was very, very *unlucky* – she was a *likho* – but she didn't say that.

Elvira set aside the black *dalmatica* and then clasped Klavdiya's hand. The girl's fingers were almost painfully warm. "My lady, I am sure there are ways to sway Lord Gavriil's heart. The red dress is an excellent start. But perhaps think of things that Lord Gavriil seems to like?"

"I have tried," Klavdiya intimated. "But he has no preferences."

"He is being polite," Elvira said. "Everyone has preferences. Has he laughed?"

At me. "No." She paused. "Well, he said he laughed in joy when I gave him flowers."

“Gifts!” Elvira said. “Gifts are perfect for swaying a man’s sentiment. We can think of gifts to give him. Flowers are excellent. I can collect some from the garden today after packing your clothes. I’ll think about other tokens you can give him.”

“Thank you,” Klavdiya said, squeezing the maid’s hand. “If the gifts work, I will make sure you never have to wear red again.”

CHAPTER 10
Rusalki

The first day on the road to Snegograd was long and waterlogged, filled with rain and mud. The Makovy train consisted of Gavriil's carriage, a pair of wagons with supplies, and a retinue of guards on horseback. The carriages and wagons struggled across the muddy roads as springtime water pelted down from the thick, gray clouds overhead, while the riders and horses simply looked miserable. They passed few people or animals on the road because most decided to remain indoors. The caravan traveled through farm- and scrubland and then through sparse forest; and the rain did not let up.

Through the forest, the Krasny River ran east to west like a twisting viper, separating Makovy from its northern neighbor Nebesnaya. The spring rains had flooded the river and overflown the bridge, so the caravan crept eastward along the riverside until they reached a barge crossing that was simple but looked safe and efficient enough to Klavdiya. Gavriil's friend Mikhail Petrovich negotiated a fare and then the process of carting the carriage and wagons individually across the river began.

"The *rusalki* are upset." Klavdiya watched the green-haired women swim up to the barge and push at its sides. The boat rocked dangerously, but thankfully it was heavy and not so easy for the water spirits to move.

Gavriil hesitated a moment too long, fear flickering in his gaze before he could hide it. Klavdiya had insisted that she was no *ved'ma*, lying and saying that she could sense magic and that was all. Nothing about being a *likho* trapped in a woman's body. But her bridegroom clearly found even that amount of magic unsettling. He put on a good face, though.

He gestured vaguely at the river. "I'm sure the *rusalki*'s home is in disarray with all this flooding."

Klavdiya nodded. The rising brown waters certainly made the water spirits more volatile, but she sensed that the *rusalki* were angry for something else. She picked at the clasp on the silver cuff on her hand as the barge rocked sharply, pushed back and forth by the *rusalki*. The cuff clicked open just as the carriage rolled off of the barge and onto the sandy shore on Nebesnaya's side of the river. As the barge rowed back towards the Makovy side, Klavdiya pressed the door handle and let herself out.

"My lady, you'll catch a cold," Gavriil protested.

"I need a few moments." She climbed down the step awkwardly, still not used to getting in or out of carriages, and then headed towards the riverside as the raid soaked through the shoulders of her *dalmatica* and *rubakha* almost immediately..

A *rusalka* beached herself on the shore, her green hair almost appearing blonde and her claws turning into small, almond-shaped nails. Out of the water, she might easily be mistaken for a beautiful human woman.

Klavdiya held out the silver cuff, rainwater trickling across its intricately carved surface.

The *rusalka* and her sisters still in the river began to laugh. "A *likho* making an offering to *rusalki*?"

"These are my humans," Klavdiya said, hoping that Gavriil could not hear her over the rush of the rain. "Take the silver as an offering and let these humans pass."

"Wouldn't you prefer a human or two to drown?" the *rusalka* asked. "It would be very bad luck."

As though summoned, Klavdiya's magic wrapped around her with a soft hiss. This time, it did not lash out – for which she was grateful. She needed Gavriil in order to break her curse and – given how he had ridden out to help her and Antonina Antonovna when their carriage broke – he would endanger himself again to help one of his own retinue. She didn't need him getting sicker or being one of the humans who fell prey to the *rusalki.*

"Take the cuff," the *likho* said.

The *rusalka* shrugged and plucked the silver bracelet from Klavdiya's hand. "If you insist."

The *rusalka* receded into the water; and she and her sisters ducked beneath the surface and disappeared. The first wagon had an easier barge ride than Klavdiya and Gavriil had had.

Wiping rain off of her face, Klavdiya climbed back into the carriage.

"You are soaked, my lady." Gavriil unbuttoned his caftan and then draped it across Klavdiya's shoulders.

He was left in a light tunic with a loose collar. Klavdiya's mouth went dry as her gaze lingered on the skin stretched across his collarbone, the way it looked so soft and... She reached out, her hand finding his chest. He was both hard and soft at once. Her pulse skipped a beat, and his eyes widened ever so slightly.

"You're so ... warm," she murmured.

"And you're freezing." He took her hand between his and began rubbing. "You shouldn't have gone out in this rain."

"The *rusalki* were trying to overturn the barge," she said. "I could make them stop."

"You are a *boyarynya,*" Gavriil whispered. "You should let others take care of you rather than running head-first into danger."

She wrapped her fingers around his. "I will not let you be hurt."

"I appreciate the sentiment, my lady," he said. "But *I* should ensure that you are not hurt."

"Who takes care of you?" she asked.

"I have a whole house of servants." Gavriil bent his head forward and kissed her knuckles. Then, he retreated back to his bench.

Klavdiya let her hand fall into her lap, but she still watched the skin over his clavicle and wondered how warm and soft it would be.

The two carriages and the retinue of mounted guards had

made the crossing. Gavriil rapped rhythmically on the roof of the carriage, signaling the driver to move on. Klavdiya watched out the window as they rolled away from the river and the handsomely-paid bargeman.

CHAPTER 11

Women's Desire

The second day of travel from Makovy to Snegograd was not nearly as miserable as the first. While the clouds remained gray and heavy, there was no rain and the sun managed to peek through here and there. Gavriil leaned an elbow against the carriage window, his cheek on his fist. He half-watched the forest turn into scrubland where deer darted between measly bushes.

He also half-watched his wife, who stared out the same window and looked incredibly bored. She had intimated to him *and Mikhail Petrovich* that she could sense magic. She wasn't a *ved'ma*, she assured him. He had never heard of a person being able to sense magic but not wield it. But for access to Snegograd's firebirds, he was willing to tolerate almost any strangeness from his wife. A missing eye? Gray-hued skin? An affinity for black? A bit of witchcraft? All of it, fine.

Mikhail was not so sympathetic. Gavriil had had an earful about Mikhail's suspicions back at Makovy, and he was sure he was due for another.

But what did Gavriil *really* have to fear from his wife? He was dying already. The only thing she could truly do was hasten it. Perhaps politick to name one of her relatives *boyar* after he passed.

Gavriil shook his head minutely.

I will not let you be hurt. He had not felt more tired or unwell than usual since her arrival – suggesting that she was *not* poisoning him. And as for politicking, she was much too blunt to be maneuvering. No, he was certain that his wife was being honest about everything.

He placed a hand on his chest where she had touched him yesterday. He could almost feel her hand, how it was cold through his tunic. He remembered the way she stared at him. He took a deep breath, focusing on the bushes outside. He knew that look in her eyes. He was no stranger to women's desire. He was a *boyar* with significant wealth, blessed with a handsome face and lean body. Before he had fallen ill, he had relished the attention of *boyarynas*, *grafinas*, baronesses, and other noblewomen.

Now, that all seemed so shallow.

Now, he wished that Klavdiya had not looked at him that way. Yes, he was her husband, but he was using their marriage, not seeking a love-match. She should not grieve for a man who used her as a tool.

Before Gavriil could dip too deep into melancholy, Mikhail Petrovich rode up alongside the window. He signaled for a rest, and Gavriil nodded. It was just after noon. The horses and people could take their respite and perhaps some food as well.

They stopped along a relatively flat stretch of land alongside the road, letting the horses graze and pick leaves off the bushes. Gavriil climbed from the carriage and then assisted Klavdiya down. Mikhail looked as though he wanted to talk, and Gavriil was about to go to him when Klavdiya grabbed his arm.

"I want to speak with you," she said.

She had had the entire carriage ride, and she wanted to speak now? Gavriil smoothed his features. "What would you like to talk about, my lady?"

She tugged on his arm, leading him a half-dozen feet away from the main group. She did not let go of him, almost hugging his arm. "I know I am not what your people hoped for."

Gavriil glanced at Mikhail and then rested his gaze on Klavdiya. "My lady, do not worry what they–"

"But please," she whispered, "I will try. I will be … whatever … you and your people want."

"My lady–"

"I know I am missing a second eye." Her fingers tightened on his arm, her expression open and tragic. "I know I say things that make you feel strange."

"You don't make me feel–"

"It is why you laugh when I am serious," she said.

He swallowed. Perhaps. He hadn't known how to accept flowers – no one had ever given him flowers – so he had laughed when taking them. When she accused him of wanting a common bride, he laughed because he didn't know what to say. And when he was blushing and she told him he was turning red, that was embarrassing.

"I will do better," she said. "I will be the wife that you want."

"I don't have some archetype–"

"Please," she said. "Don't discard me. I know that is what Mikhail Petrovich advises. Please, don't."

Gavriil licked his lips. How did she know what he and Mikhail spoke about in private? Or had she guessed?

"I will learn," she insisted. "I will be a good wife. One you will love."

Love. Klavdiya wanted love. Gavriil wanted hunting rights. A pang pricked his heart. He needed to turn her away from such ideas. He did not deserve her affections. And ... he did not know if he could even give her what she wanted. The only thing he had cared about for the two years was curing himself. He doubted he remembered much more than self-preservation.

He put his hand over hers. As always, it was bitterly cold and he had a strong desire to hold it close in order to warm it. He resisted the urge. "I promised I would cherish you as my wife, and I will."

Disappointment painted Klavdiya's features. Slowly, she let go of his arm. He missed the feel of her fingers. She glanced over her shoulder and then back. "You will tell Mikhail Petrovich that you will keep me?"

"I always do, my lady," he assured her. She turned to leave, but this time he caught her by the elbow. "Know that I am pleased with this marriage, my lady."

Because I got what I wanted from it.

Klavdiya nodded and then slipped away.

Gavriil stood outside the caravan circle for a moment longer, watching his bride go to her lady's maid. The two bowed their heads in conversation. He sighed and twisted the red yarn at his throat. He would never be the man to love her, only the man that needed her.

CHAPTER 12

Snegograd

Ruled by a suspicious and arrogant man, Snegograd remained in isolation from the rest of the Rodgorodian province; and because of its isolation, walking through its halls felt like stepping into a painting of a time nearly thirty years past. Over supper, Lord Roman and Lady Antonina interrogated Gavriil while making silly statements like "Oh, that's our Klavdiya." Klavdiya sat silently. She was still perturbed by how strong Baba Les's spell was, to last this long and still convince two parents that a *likho* was their child. Past midnight, the Lord and Lady of Snegograd finally released Klavdiya and Gavriil to their guestroom.

Gavriil caught the edge of the settee and slumped, running a hand across his face.

Klavdiya's magic snapped in warning, reacting to his natural misfortune. She went to his side, taking his arm.

"Call my valet," Gavriil said. "He will prepare me for bed."

"I will help."

He shook his head. "Ladies don't trouble themselves with–"

"You are my husband," Klavdiya said. Elvira had coached her to be more forthcoming – in hopes that Gavriil simply needed things stated plainly, that then he might understand that she needed more from him than politeness. "I will help you."

He sighed, clearly giving up. He straightened, though his face was pale and his eyes ringed by dark circles.

Klavdiya gave him a grateful glance and then began swiftly unbuttoning his caftan. Next came the tunic. She ground her teeth, wondering why she liked the look of his chest in the moonlight. She was a *likho;* and she should not find a human ... beautiful. She guided him towards the bed, where he removed his own boots.

"I'll keep the trousers." His voice wavered as he said it. He gestured weakly to the other side of the bed. "You may lie there if you wish. I won't touch you."

Touch her? Like hold her hand or...? Klavdiya frowned as Gavriil crawled into bed. Then, she walked to the side of the bed and lay on it. This was the closest, she realized, that he'd ever allowed. So close that she could feel the heat from him. Her gaze raked over him.

"You are bruised," she said, gesturing to the blemishes covering his arms and one particularly large one blooming across his right shoulder.

His eyes fell closed. "It's the blood miasma."

One of her fists curled around the blankets, and her magic hissed. The fire in the hearth spluttered and almost went out. Yes, he had told her he was sick, but this was the first symptom she had seen. She could not let him die.

Awkwardly resting her head against the pillow, she reached over and gripped his hand. "I need you."

He did not respond, his breathing slow and deep from slumber.

In the dark, she lay barely a pace from him, her fingers curled over his. As a *likho*, she did not need to sleep, so instead she remained silent and still with her own thoughts. *Know that I am pleased with this marriage*. His words from earlier in the day cut her. Elvira told her to explain herself, and Klavdiya had. But that did not change Gavriil. He was as far from loving her as the first day they met. And she would never be free of Baba Les's spell.

Gavriil stirred with the dawn. He turned his face to her, his gaze bleary. "Did you sleep at all?"

"A little," she lied.

"We're going to travel onward into Snegograd's wilderness," he murmured. "You'll need your rest."

"I've never slept much."

He nodded minutely and then said, "Thank you. For last night."

She reached out and let her finger trace around one of the bruises on his arm. He looked back at her strangely. "How bad is it?" she asked. "The sickness."

"I get tired easily, and my bones hurt all the time," he said. "I bruise easily and sometimes my skin gets these red pinpricks all over. The physicians thought I would die within six months. It's been two years."

Panic lanced through her. She had no time. He could die at any moment. He had to love her before it was too late. "You are strong."

"Lucky, maybe." He shrugged.

Unlucky, she thought, to be married to a *likho.*

"I am desperate for that firebird," Gavriil said. "Their feathers are known for all manner of curative properties. If anything can cure me, it's a firebird feather." He was quiet for a long moment. "I don't want to die."

"I don't want you to die." It was the most honest thing she had ever said. "We will find the firebird."

"I don't profess to understand how you can sense magic but not be a *ved'ma,*" he said. "But I don't care. If you can help me, I will give you anything you want."

"You will love me?"

"Rodú, I probably will," he said. "I can't promise you romantic love, my lady. I don't believe that exists for me. But I will adore you for saving my life."

She drew her hand away. Were there different types of love? She didn't know. Surely, a *likho* couldn't love. But did humans love in many ways? If they did, would any type of love satisfy Baba Les? Klavdiya should have asked, but it was a question she had not known existed.

"I know that isn't what you want." Gavriil propped himself up on an elbow. "After finding the firebird and after producing two heirs, I will allow you to take lovers. You can have your romance, your great love."

"There's only you." Klavdiya plucked lint off the woolen blankets. Lovers would not change her back into a *likho*. "Whatever ... type ... of love you can offer must be enough."

"You might change your mind, my lady," he said. "I would not blame you."

CHAPTER 13

The Vikhr

Not far afield from the Snegograd manor, one of the carriage horses pulled a shoe. They sent a messenger for Snegograd's farrier to come replace the shoe, but for now, the caravan remained stuck in place. Gavriil folded his arms and tapped his foot, wanting to get out into Snegograd's fields where the firebirds were rumored to nest. Here was the shrubland in which Snegograd's manor lay – a land of short bushes that grew a variety of berries. This time of year, the winter berries were shriveled and falling off the stem, while the summer berries were nothing more than tiny green buds. All of it lay beneath muted gray clouds.

Across from him, Klavdiya was examining her fingernails, which were cut shorter than most ladies preferred. *There's only you.* Gavriil shifted in his seat, which creaked. Klavdiya did not look up. She wasn't what he had expected in a noble bride, but she was determined and sweet and, yes, blunt. And even if he hated to admit it, he liked her. It just wasn't love and never could be; Gavriil didn't fall in love. She shouldn't waste her time on a man who was using her either.

"I should go outside," Klavdiya announced and then pulled the handle, letting herself out of the carriage.

A bit dumbfounded, Gavriil watched her walk a good distance away. The wind grabbed at her skirts, ruffling them like dark waves on a black lake. She turned northward, hugging herself, and squinted into the distance.

Climbing from the carriage, Gavriil called to the footman for his and Klavdiya's coats. He pulled on his outerwear and then headed to his wife, laying the coat over her shoulders.

"I do not get as cold as you." She gave him a sidelong glance. A faint breeze tugged at her cap and intricately-done braids. "But thank you."

"I should tell you to go back to the carriage," he said. "But I am guessing that you have some reason you came out here. No *rusalki*, I hope. There's no water."

"I'm looking for magic." She pulled on the coat. "I see traces but not of a firebird."

Gavriil rubbed the back of his neck where his hairs stood on end. He might never get used to her uncanny abilities. "What traces do you see?"

"A *vikhr*."

A whirlwind. A wind spirit rumored to bring wind so strong that they could lift a man off his feet and carry him a mile. "Hopefully headed away from us."

Klavdiya squinted. Not a good sign.

The shadows darkened around her, crawling towards and then up her skirts. Gavriil staggered forward. His hand found her waist just as the shadows did. She was cold, her fine wool *dalmatica* soft to the touch. The shadows were pure ice, lancing his fingers down to the bone. Gooseflesh puckered his skin as the shadows curled around his hands and wrists. *Magic*. Whether she knew it or not, his wife had magic. His hold on her tightened. He needed her, regardless.

A drop of blood splattered on his shoe. *Rodú*. Another bloody nose. With his free hand, he pulled out his handkerchief and blotted his nose.

The shadow slithered around Klavdiya like a second skin, crackling with something akin to black electricity. Then, slowly, it receded until she seemed nothing more than a noblewoman looking into the distance.

She turned to him, then, glancing down at his hand on her ribs before meeting his gaze. "The *vikhr* is headed towards us."

"High winds!" Gavriil shouted. "Hold the horses! Stake the carriages!" He took her hand. "Come, my lady."

They reached the carriage just as the first gale struck. The carriage horses reared and plunged. The driver, the footman, and the farrier held on as fast as they could. Gavriil yanked the carriage door open, gesturing for Klavdiya to enter. Then, another gale hit. Gavriil and Klavdiya collided with the side of the carriage, which teetered. A third gust knocked the carriage off its wheels and onto its side with a spitting *crack*. The horses screamed. One got loose. Gavriil grabbed Klavdiya and yanked her out of the way as a chunk of harness came flying backwards over the toppled carriage. Behind them, the other horses panicked; and everyone fought to keep the wagons upright.

Gavriil and Klavdiya hauled themselves off the top of the carriage and into the dirt. Gavriil wrapped his arm around Klavdiya and pulled her face into his chest, protecting her from flying debris. Through the roaring wind, he heard laughter. The *vikhr* was *laughing* at their misery.

"Stop!" he shouted. "We're just trying to pass through!"

"Bad luck clings to you," said the voice in the wind.

"I *know*," Gavriil said. "I'm dying."

The *vikhr* laughed and blew.

"Let us go!" he asked again.

"Learn to love your *likho*," the *vikhr* said, its tempest twisting tighter and faster. "Only when you stop fighting does she let go."

Then, the *vikhr* swept away, frighting the horses one last time before it disappeared westward. The air filled with the sound of men and women calming the horses. Trembling, his nose still bleeding, Gavriil held tightly to his wife for a long moment. Even through her clothes, she felt cold – like she had been dipped in a cold lake. Likely from fear.

He squeezed her shoulders. "We're all right, my lady."

"The *likho*–" she stammered.

"I'm not surprised," he said and she paled. "Of course, I would be cursed by a *likho*. It's probably a *likhoradka*, a spirit of disease. That's why I have this blood miasma."

Klavdiya was still in his arms, her expression unreadable.

"The *vikhr* said you must love her."

Slowly, Gavriil let go of her and stood. He helped her to her feet, holding her hands tightly once they were both on their feet. "It's from the children's tale, right? You don't know it?"

She shook her head.

"There were two men. The first was tricked by a *likho* and had to carry her around his neck," Gavriil explained. "He decided to drown the *likho* and so jumped into a river. Unfortunately, he only drowned himself; the *likho* floated away.

"The *likho* then tricked the second man and he had to carry her around his neck," he continued. "But this man gave her gifts – heels of bread and berries that he had foraged – that made the *likho* happy. Eventually, she had mercy on him and left."

Klavdiya's grip was white-knuckle tight on his hands.

"Don't worry, my lady," he said. "I am used to ill-luck. I certainly will not drown myself. I will simply have to be kinder to bad luck."

CHAPTER 14

My Love's Embrace

Folding her legs in front of her, Klavdiya propped her chin on her hands, her elbows on her knees and stared across the camp to where Gavriil spoke with Mikhail Petrovich and the hunters. In the dark, with the campfire light painting him in tones of gold and red, Gavriil did not look as tired as he usually did. Klavdiya knew that she gave him nosebleeds, but did she cause him fatigue? Certainly, he had had the blood miasma before Klavdiya; she wasn't making him sick.

She ran the fairy tale through her mind again. Baba Les had made her curse to fit that damned story perfectly. The more Gavriil fought Klavdiya's affections, the stronger the binds imprisoning Klavdiya were. The kinder he was, the looser.

And if he loved her...

"Still thinking about your husband, my lady?" Elvira sat before their small, shared fire, darning a pair of socks. She looked a bit like a fire fairy, bright red in the firelight.

Klavdiya nodded.

"Before the *vikhr* attacked, I saw him put his arm around your waist," the maid said. "That is progress."

She didn't need him to touch her. "I need him to love me."

"Touching shows affection or yearning," Elvira said. "Either could turn into love."

Klavdiya turned abruptly towards her maid. "What do you mean?"

The maid snorted. Klavdiya could not tell if it was in amusement or some other emotion. "You know how you have to build affection through gift giving? It is the same through touch. And with enough affection, sometimes there is love. Were you really so sheltered that you don't know any of this?"

"I know nothing of love," Klavdiya said truthfully. A *likho* didn't love.

Elvira sighed and glanced over to where Gavriil sat. "This must be difficult for you, not knowing anything."

"You know," Klavdiya said. "How did you learn?"

"Everyone talks about it." The maid flushed. "Well, serfs and peasants talk about it."

Klavdiya rubbed her face. Baba Les had given her an impossible task.

"Well, make sure to stand close enough to him that he can touch you," her maid recommended. "So that it's *easy* for him to touch you. You could give him little touches – a touch on the arm or hand."

Klavdiya scowled. Gavriil was always touching her hands. She remembered placing her hand on his chest after bargaining with the *rusalki*. When he had taken off his caftan to keep her warm. He had been in such a thin tunic that she could see the planes of his chest. She closed her fist. Her palm tingled just thinking about it.

Elvira folded and then tucked the socks into her apron pocket. She stood. "It's late, my lady, and there's another day of travel ahead of us. Let's get you to bed."

Another night of sitting awake in the carriage. Klavdiya knew better than to argue. She let the young woman take her to the far side of the carriage and prepare her for bed – removing the dalmatica and changing into a cloud-soft, dove-gray *rubakha* that served as her nightdress. The maid unpinned her cap and braids, letting Klavdiya's ink-black hair fall to her waist. Then, Elvira helped her into the carriage, arranging the pillows behind her.

Finally, Klavdiya was alone and staring at the carriage's cracked window. When she touched it, the crack grew longer and more spidery. She drew her finger away.

She reclined, folding her legs alongside her, on the bench.

She had learned over the past few days that sitting upright all night perturbed Gavriil. When she reclined, he seemed to lie to himself about her need to sleep.

How long would it be before he realized she wasn't human?

And did she want that?

After perhaps an hour alone, Gavriil entered the carriage, wearing only loose trousers and a simple tunic. No silver at his throat or on his fingers. Still, her human heart flickered when she saw him.

"Not asleep yet, my lady?" he whispered.

"I am not tired," she said, knowing she should have pretended to sleep.

"The *vikhr* was rough," he said. "I would expect many of us will have trouble sleeping tonight."

"The *likho*..."

The vikhr *told you to love your* likho, she wanted to say. *Your likho is me.*

But Gavriil thought his *likho* made him sick – and Klavdiya did not. If she played to his fears, he might love her. But he would cease his hunt for the firebird, and then he would die. A *likho* should not care whether a human died, but Klavdiya cared if Gavriil did.

"I'm not scared of bad luck," Gavriil said. "I live with it every day."

A pang bloomed deep in her chest. Could he love it – *her* – like the *vikhr* said?

He did not answer her unspoken question, remaining quiet for a long moment. He propped his head on his fist, his gaze soft. The moonlight filtered through the window, shattering as it hit the crack in the glass and glimmering in a thousand pieces across Gavriil's skin. He was beautiful, Klavdiya thought, in the way the night sky was – dark and filled with sparkling stars. She wanted to cross the gap between the two benches and touch him just as Elvira had recommended. Instead, she remained still, watching him in return.

"This reminds me of a poem," Gavriil said.

"When stars be shimm'ring sharp and night be cold,
So comes my love's embrace tender and bold.
Lo, kisses, kisses– I do beg twofold,
That she may allow our love to take hold."

He held out his hand. "Give me your hand, my lady."

She reached out and settled her fingers in his. Slowly, carefully as though she were made of thin ice, he pressed a kiss to her knuckles and then to her palm.

"You don't believe in love," Klavdiya said.

"No." He did not let go of her hand. "But it's a beautiful poem." He sighed. "Klavdiya, you are beautiful."

She found herself laughing. "I have one eye."

"A beautiful eye," he said. "And hair like midnight-colored ink, skin that looks like quicksilver in the moonlight. A more talented man might write a poem about you. Perhaps I will hire a bard to write a poem about you when we return to Makovy."

Her throat constricted. "I only want a poem written by you."

"It will be a miserable poem, my lady," he said. "I am a reciter, not a writer."

She slid from her bench, landing gently on her knees. Her fingers found the impeccably soft wool of his tunic as she traced her way up his chest. He smelled of rosemary and a day on the road. He sighed, leaning his head forward. And then, she pressed her mouth to his.

A deep chasm opened inside her, begging for ... something. It was hungry, it *wanted*. She pulled away quickly, terrified of feeding the hunger.

Gavriil gazed back at her, his features soft. He ran a finger along her cheek. "You're beautiful, Klavdiya. I swear it. But this cannot be. Not now."

Wordlessly, she receded back to her bench. The hunger was gone and now all she felt was empty.

CHAPTER 15

No Other Name

Klavdiya's magic was growing more erratic, more uncontrollable. The same horse had lost a second shoe, forcing the driver to pull all four of its shoes because they were too far to call the farrier. Then, with an errant snap of her magic, the food in the wagons spoiled prematurely, forcing the caravan to seek out a serf settlement in order to barter for more supplies.

This particular settlement was little more than two cottages and three barns – all made of scraps of wood and roofed with thatch. The extended family which lived here grew barley and hardy vegetables like cabbage, onions, and beets, while also husbanding a pair of cows and a handful of sheep. Gavriil muttered his doubts about the serfs having enough to sell, but still they approached.

They were greeted by a man named Vaarlam Osipovich. Vaarlam was short and thin with a mop of curly, red hair. He was missing three fingers on his left hand. He pointed with his remaining fingers. "You have soldiers."

"We mean no harm. We're hoping to buy supplies. Food." Gavriil held his coat tightly around him. His skin was sallow and his eyes were ringed with dark circles. Klavdiya clenched and unclenched her fists as she hovered near the carriage, watching Gavriil and Mikhail Petrovich attempt to negotiate. The travel wore on Gavriil. She did not know how long he could go before he truly put his health at risk.

Vaarlam shook his head. "We need protection."

Mikhail Petrovich scowled. "You need to call upon the Lord

of Snegograd. This is the Lord of Makovy. We are just passing through."

"We only need a few armed men, please," the serf said, clasping his hands before him as though in prayer.

Gavriil began to agree with Mikhail, "It would be better if Lord Roman–"

"Please, my lords!" Vaarlam fell to his knees, holding his clasped hands aloft. "It's a *striga*!"

Klavdiya crept forward, scanning the settlement once again. She had not been looking for magic – or signs of the undead – but now that she looked, she saw the faint and twisted trail of ... something. The trail was dark gold and black and smudged like ink that a child had run a wet finger over. Whether the creature was a *striga* or some other monster, she was not sure. Not from her vantage point, at least.

Gavriil looked over his shoulder at her. She nodded once.

"And you have told your lord that there is a *striga*?" Gavriil asked.

"Yes, my lord," Vaarlam said. "We have not received help."

"Gavrik, we cannot spend our time chasing ghosts," Mikhail said. "We have a mission. This is Snegograd's responsibility."

"These are Klavdiya's people, Misha," Gavriil said. "And they need our help."

Klavdiya stepped forward. A *likho* ought not care that a *striga* walked the land, but Gavriil needed food and rest – and these people might offer it. And she was more equipped to handle a *striga* than any mortal. "I will find the *striga*."

Gavriil turned to Vaarlam. "We will handle the *striga* if you will give us any food you can spare."

"You will let Lord Gavriil Gavriilovich sleep in the house," Klavdiya amended.

Vaarlam glanced between the two of them and then nodded. "Yes, my lord. Yes, my lady. You can avail yourself of all our hospitality. Please, let me show your people where you can board your horses and where your retinue can stay. My wife can show you to a quiet space in the house, my lord."

Gavriil inclined his head, and Vaarlam set about his task. Vaarlam's wife showed Klavdiya and Gavriil to an empty corner of the larger cottage and then supplied them with blankets.

Klavdiya helped her husband to sit. "I must wait until night. The *striga* sleeps during the day."

"I will go with you," Gavriil said.

"No."

"I cannot let my lady wife face a monster alone," he protested.

"You are getting worse," she said.

He winced as though she had struck him. Then, he sighed and ran a hand over his face. "I know. But as I said, I can't let you go alone." He swallowed visibly. "Let me send Mikhail Petrovich with you. I know you and he… But I trust him. And he knows what he is doing."

Reluctantly, she agreed.

Klavdiya remained in the cottage most of the day, while Gavriil dozed. The physician and the nun came to see him, rousing him for his daily medicine and prayers respectively. Mikhail Petrovich came to watch over him as well, giving Klavdiya some reprieve during the afternoon in which she wandered the settlement and followed the *striga*'s trail. It headed westward out towards the barley fields.

Mikhail Petrovich was leaning against the wall, examining the fletching on his arrows, when she returned. His expression was stormy; and he gestured to Gavriil, who slept. "He's dying and you want to go on some ghost-hunt."

"He needed the rest and we needed the food," she replied.

"Who *are* you?" In two steps, Mikhail crossed the distance between them. He towered over Klavdiya, one of his white-blonde tresses slipping in front of his eyes. "*Boyars* don't marry off one-eyed girls; and the noblewomen certainly don't offer to slay monsters. I *know* you aren't Klavdiya Romanovna."

"I have no other name." It wasn't a lie. If she was not Klavdiya, she was just the *likho*.

"Then you are not Lord Roman Avdeyevich and Lady Antonina Antonovich's daughter," he accused.

"You have told Gavriil this." She stared up at him, refusing to even blink. "And he does not believe it."

"He is too soft-hearted," Mikhail growled. "But I cannot let him be a fool."

"I am Klavdiya Romanovna and I am married to Lord Gavriil Gavriilovich," she said. "He is a *boyar*. What are you?"

A muscle in Mikhail's jaw twitched as he turned bright red. "Do not pull rank on me, you–"

"Misha." Gavriil sat, rubbing at one of his eyes. "You will respect my wife and your *boyarynya*."

Mikhail Petrovich's teeth clicked as he shut his mouth, the insult silenced.

Klavdiya gave Mikhail Petrovich an evil grin. When she returned to her *likho* form, he would be the first person she cursed. Then, she sidestepped the lesser lord and went to her husband.

CHAPTER 16

The Striga

The moon hung low, a thin sliver of white-silver against a still blue sky, when Klavdiya left the settlement with a coat, a small belt knife, and a hawthorne stake. She needed neither, but the humans would not understand that. Stalking several paces behind her came Mikhail Petrovich, armed with a bow and arrow as well as a beat-up shortsword.

The *striga*'s trail was even fainter than before, mostly washed away by a late afternoon rain. Klavdiya found a trace of the *striga* lurking beneath the second cottage's window. Diffused prints climbed the wall and onto the roof, but the *striga* was no longer there – and so Klavdiya did not pursue that trail. Instead, she searched the ground for more tracks. Several paces to the west and towards the granary another mark – flickering gold and black – scraped against the ground. She crouched, running her fingers across the surface of the mud. A trickle of magic caressed hers.

"There's a patch of mud on the roof there." Mikhail pointed to the granary.

"She is using her wings to glide." Klavdiya said and then walked around the barn. A shimmer of gold looped over the roof's apex and down the other side. She pointed to another patch of mud, where the grass had been scraped away. "She landed here."

Following the fragments of magic as well as the scraped away grass, Klavdiya and Mikhail headed westward. They passed the settlement's well and then past the tree line planted as a windbreak. The land then sloped downward, the ground turning rocky and the *striga*'s scraping becoming less and less apparent on the harder ground. Klavdiya almost lost its trail twice before finding a blur of black and gold that continued through a copse of dying linden trees. As the night turned indigo, they came upon a small, flat stretch of land covered by ash.

Mikhail bent and picked up a handful. "Someone died and not too long ago. These are ashes from a funeral pyre."

"*Striga* aren't born from the fire," Klavdiya said.

"No." He let the ash sift through his fingers, floating away on a faint breeze. "They arise when someone *isn't* burned. So, the question isn't whose pyre this is, but who else died? We can find her and put a stake through her. We can go back and ask the serfs."

Klavdiya was about to agree with him. Surely, the serfs knew who and where their missing dead was, the woman who had not received proper funerary rites.

Then, Mikhail Petrovich collapsed.

A shadow preened itself atop him – a woman, warped beyond recognition, with bat wings instead of arms. She shrieked so piercingly that Klavdiya could feel the sound reverberating inside her bones. The *striga* lifted a wing that ended in a claw, about to slash Mikhail's throat. He thrust his sword upward and into her belly. She screeched again, toppling sideways. Blood splattered from her mouth as she staggered after Mikhail, who had rolled away from her and onto his feet. The wound in her belly sealed on its own.

Klavdiya reached for her magic, only for it to slip out of her grasp. She growled, running towards the *striga*. She struck the *striga* – a full-body tackle – before the creature could wallop Mikhail. She and the *striga* rolled across the ashen and rocky ground. She grabbed for her knife. The *striga* grabbed her wrist and twisted. Klavdiya cried out as something popped and her hand went numb. The knife toppled out of its sheath and onto the ground, useless unless she could grab it with her other hand. But the *striga* had her good hand in its mouth, sinking its teeth into her flesh.

The *striga* reeled back, spitting out inky, black blood, giving Klavdiya the moment she needed to scramble back.

Her head spun when she put weight on her wrist, and she almost vomited. This human body was weak. Her vision blurring, she grabbed the stake with her good hand and yanked it free of the belt.

The *striga* rounded on Mikhail, who likely had better-tasting blood to eat. She circled around the nobleman, slurring in a language that Klavdiya did not recognize. Keeping his sword between himself and the monster, Mikhail struggled to keep the *striga* in front of him, to prevent her from getting behind him again. Blood seeped down the back of his skull, staining his blond hair. He threw a strike; and the *striga* evaded, her body twisting like vines. The monster lunged. Mikhail parried – barely. She struck again, this time knocking him to the ground. He kept the sword between them. She tore, clawed, grappled, and gnashed. She was too close for a sword; he kicked her in the chest.

Her good arm shaking, Klavdiya raised the stake.

The *striga* beat her wings and lifted off the ground. Her attacks came from odd angles as she swooped in on him. Her claw tore through his shoulder. Dark blood soaked the ground.

"You stupid bitch," Mikhail snarled.

The *striga* fell with a terrible *crack*. Mikhail cursed again. The *striga* bent her head forward and began to drink from his shoulder.

Klavdiya was moving forward. Her magic crackled around her, but she couldn't control it. It was a dark cloud and pulsing electricity. She brought the stake down. The wood pierced through the *striga*'s back, parting her gold-gray skin. The monster howled and swung around, knocking Klavdiya with its wing. Klavdiya hit the dirt, landing on her bad arm. She puked. She couldn't see straight. The *striga* was coming for her.

Then, the monster fell flat on its face.

CHAPTER 17

An Ill Omen

Mikhail Petrovich had a broken arm, two broken ribs, and multiple lacerations – precipitating his return to Makovy with two guards. On the other hand, Klavdiya was "lucky," having only a broken wrist that she wore close to her chest in a sling. Already, her magic festered about the break, mending it.

From the settlement, beyond the treeline, she could see a fire blazing. The serfs were burning the *striga*. Cradling her bad arm, Klavdiya watched the orange glow above the treeline from a secluded place behind the granary.

A rock skittered across the ground.

She raised her gaze, meeting Gavriil's. He approached. "How is my warrior wife, killer of *striga*?"

"Why do they burn her?" Klavdiya asked.

"So she cannot come back," he said. "They should have burned her when she first died. But they thought she was unclean because she had killed herself." He shook his head sadly. "It is rare but without the proper funeral rites, dead women can become *striga* and men *upiór*. My father dealt with an *upiór* when I was a child; otherwise, I might not believe it."

Klavdiya nodded. That a human could come back from the dead – she had never thought about it before.

"Klavdiya, when I am gone, I do not want you to–" Gavriil lifted a hand, brushed her cheek with his fingertips. "My mother sacrificed herself when my father died, wishing to join him in the world beyond. She saw it as her duty as a wife. I know that some see it as the greatest honor a noblewoman can have, to die for her husband. But I do not want that. I want you to live your life."

"You will not die," she said. "Not soon."

He cupped her face. "I do not know that. This hunt might all be for naught. I might not catch a firebird, or its feathers might not cure me."

Her hand settled on his chest, his caftan silken beneath her fingers. His palm against her cheek was warm, and she leaned into it. He *could* not die. Not just because she would be trapped under Baba Les's spell, but because… "I would miss you."

"I would miss you, too, Klavdiya." He released a shaking breath. "I did not mean for it to be this way. I meant for our marriage to be a convenience, a way to gain access to your father's lands. I didn't realize my bride would be bold, intelligent, funny, and even strong. I didn't expect to–" He looped an arm around her, drawing her closer. "I didn't expect to want you."

"You may want me." Klavdiya's human heart fluttered, and her throat constricted. These weren't the sensations belonging to a *likho*, not one who only cared about finding her freedom.

"I might die," he whispered. "I will break your heart. And it'll break mine to leave you. I cannot love you."

You must, she willed.

"But Rodú, I want to."

Gavriil bent his head forward, tilted her face up, and then kissed her. Heat seared through her like a bolt of electricity; and her fingers tightened on his caftan. He pulled away a hairsbreadth only to kiss her again, this time slowly coaxing a deeper kiss. A moan escaped Klavdiya's throat. These were not the sounds of a *likho*. And as he held her, his lips soft yet insistent, she wondered if she was a *likho* at all anymore. Because she felt entirely human, held against his chest.

Her magic hissed, pooling around her. She willed it back, not wanting to end this moment. But then something *thump*ed on the ground beside them. A magpie. Dead. It had fallen from its perch on the roof above.

"That's an ill omen," Gavriil said, slowly releasing Klavdiya as he gazed down at the dead bird.

She hid a wince. "A coincidence."

"We've faced a *striga*, a *vikhr*, and *rusalki*," Gavriil said, guiding her by the elbow away from the granary. "I would not be surprised to find a *ved'ma* or worse on our path."

"She would certainly be easier than a *striga*," muttered Klavdiya.

Gavriil laughed. "You are not in fighting form."

"I will heal quickly," she assured him.

"I pray that is the case." His hand slid into hers. "Come, my lady, let us return to the caravan. We should travel on."

From the settlement with the *striga*, they traveled northward. The rains grew more sporadic, and the wind became violent only in the late afternoon as spring made ready for summer. The sparse trees gave way to grasslands with clusters of bushes. Wildflowers in yellow, pink, and purple blossomed in every direction, making more than a few travelers sniffle and sneeze.

On the third day of travel, a scout came galloping back. "My lord, we found a nest."

Taking the most docile horse amongst them – and it still skittered about when Klavdiya first approached it – Klavdiya rode out with Gavriil and three armsmen. About a mile ahead of the caravan, beneath the shade of some dead and leafless bushes, they found a nest on the ground. There were no eggshells nor feathers, but the nest was large enough to sleep at least two men. It was not just a common sparrow's nest.

"Is there magic here?" Gavriil asked Klavdiya.

She nodded. All around the place was smudged red and green and white magic. Whatever beast made this nest overflowed with magic; and it had been here recently. "Are firebirds this large?"

"I did not think so," her husband said. "But what else could have made such a nest?"

A laughter – so joyous that even Klavdiya felt the urge to laugh – filled the air; and a great shadow passed over them. Shielding her eye against the sun, Klavdiya looked up and saw the nest's owner.

CHAPTER 18

The Alkonost

The creature landed heavily, the ground shaking from the impact. It was a massive bird – its feathers scintillating with every color of the rainbow – with the head of a woman, her long, brown tresses streaming down around her wings. The horses snorted and shied from her. She cocked her head, blinking her yellow eyes, and then laughed.

Holding his mount steady, Gavriil gritted his teeth against the sudden urge to laugh. His heart felt open, jubilant even, as he gazed upon her. The creature was bewitching; and he knew exactly with whom he dealt. "You're the Alkonost."

She trilled – a sound that felt like delight. Gavriil clenched his fists, digging his nails into his palm to distract himself from the emotions she caused to rush through him. She sang rather than spoke, her voice like a chapel's bell. "I am the Bringer of Joy and the Messenger of the Gods. I am the Alkonost."

Klavdiya had dismounted, letting her horse skitter away to hide behind the other horses. Her dark skirts stirred, though there was no breeze, as she approached the Alkonost.

The Alkonost turned her joyous face towards Klavdiya, though her words were somber. "The gods know you are here and what you are."

"I do not believe in gods," Klavdiya answered, and the guards behind Gavriil shifted. It was not a common thing for one to denounce the gods. But his wife was brave, perhaps so brave that she could face the world without the protection of the gods.

"They have deemed you a curse," sang the bird-woman,

shaking out her multicolored wings. "They would send you away."

Dismounting, Gavriil came to stand beside his wife. He clasped her shoulder. "This is my wife, Lady Alkonost, not a curse."

"You saw Rodú's mirror break, and you heard his prophecy," the Alkonost said. "You did not heed him?"

Gavriil felt at his throat. The red yarn from their wedding still remained. A good omen. He pulled it from under his caftan and showed it to the bird-woman. "My wedding thread remains, though."

Klavdiya reached below the collar of her *rubakha* and pulled out her own yarn, still tied about her neck.

The Alkonost sat on her slender feet, tilting her head left and right as she examined the yarn. She ruffled and then smoothed her feathers. Finally, she said, "Rodú ought to have snapped those, too. I do not understand his warnings coupled with his blessings."

"Rodú must know that I am sick," Gavriil said. "And that Klavdiya was my one hope of finding a cure."

The bird-woman cooed softly, much like a dove. "What a strange thing for one's ill luck to be a blessing."

Gavriil scowled. "What do you mean–?"

The Alkonost laughed again and, despite himself, Gavriil began to laugh. His guards laughed, and even Klavdiya smiled nonsensically. Tears burned in his eyes, and he couldn't breathe because of the laughter and the pure joy pouring through him. He threaded his fingers through Klavdiya's, trying to steady himself. And only after a few minutes, did everyone sober.

It was Klavdiya who regained her composure first. "We are looking for a firebird."

The Alkonost blinked, bringing her large – if humanoid – head down to Klavdiya's level. She blinked, her eyes yellow-amber like a bird's. "What good will a firebird do you?"

Gavriil took a step forward. "It's for me. Have you not heard from the gods that I am sick? The firebird's feathers have magic; they may cure me."

The bird-woman cooed softly, straightening. "Do you not realize that you are doomed? There is no outcome that will bring you what you want."

A shiver ran up his spine, and his throat closed up. Did the Alkonost mean that ... that no matter what, Gavriil would not be cured? That he would die? Even if he caught a firebird and plucked its feathers. "There must be something I can do," he choked.

"Catch the firebird and be forever broken," the Alkonost warned. "Turn around and go home, and you will perish."

"I have to go on then," he said. "I'll be dead otherwise."

"Death may bring you what you need," said the bird-woman.

"No," Gavriil said.

"He will not die," Klavdiya said. "I will not let him."

Gavriil watched his wife from the corner of his eye. She had thrown her shoulders back and was glaring with her one black eye at the Alkonost as though she might defeat such a creature with a staring contest. And as though she might defy fate. Rodú, he hoped his wife *could* defy fate and the will of the gods. Otherwise, Gavriil would die or maybe worse.

"You are a funny creature," the Alkonost told Klavdiya, "to think you can change the twist of fate."

"I am bad luck," Klavdiya said. "I have always been able to change fate."

Much later, after having left the Alkonost behind and having returned to the caravan, Gavriil sat beside Klavdiya by the crackling campfire. Though the days grew warmer, the nights remained brisk with strong winds. He huddled in his coat with a cloak pulled over his shoulders as well. Klavdiya sat with her coat unbuttoned, the wind tossing her collar to and fro.

"You're not bad luck," Gavriil said.

Klavdiya pinched ash, smearing it between her fingers. "I am."

He clasped her hand, the hand she had not soiled with soot. "No, you have been nothing but good luck for me. I would have never expected to marry a woman as dedicated as you."

Klavdiya turned to him, cupping his cheek and besmearing his face with ash. “You cannot die. I will be left here, and I will have nothing.”

“I do not know what the Alkonost predicted when she said I would be broken.” He leaned into her hand. Why did he want her, when he had promised himself he wouldn’t? Slowly, he let himself feel for Klavdiya, to wish for something more than a few soft touches and stolen kisses. “But it will be better than dying, surely. I will– I will still be with you.”

“If you still want me when this is done,” Klavdiya said.

“Of course,” Gavriil murmured.

CHAPTER 19

The Dark and Cold

Was a *likho* supposed to feel like this? Klavdiya paced outside the carriage where Gavriil slept. The caravan slept, save for two guards who kept watch and Klavdiya. She hugged herself, rubbing her arms, though she was not cold. Instead, she felt too full as though a bright light lit within her chest, trying to escape by any means necessary.

Even after the Alkonost proclaimed this hunt for a firebird doomed.

I will still be with you.

Klavdiya sucked on her lower lip. Gavriil wanted to be with her. A *likho*! And she... She liked that. She wanted him to survive, for him to stay with her.

Because if he dies, you will never be a likho *again,* she told herself.

But why did it make her feel so ... light? She was certain, even in her most triumphant moments – when she cursed a person so perfectly – she had never known joy like this. Not when the Alkonost forced everyone to laugh. No, a *likho* didn't feel joy blazing in her chest. Klavdiya pressed her hand over the place where her heart should be. It even *felt* warm.

Then, she pressed her hand to the carriage side, closing her eye for a moment, in promise. They *would* find the firebird and Gavriil would be cured.

Quietly, she sidled around the other side of the carriage. Letting the darkness cloak her, she slipped out into the flatlands. The stars shone dimly, barely lighting the short and brittle glass.

But Klavdiya was a creature of the dark and the cold of the night; she did not need the starlight but her own, singular black eye. The world was muted – black, gray, and beige – as she navigated further and further away from the caravan. The air grew colder, prickling against her weak, human skin; and her breath turned to silver mist.

When the caravan was only the flicker of a campfire on the horizon, she stopped. The wind tousled her clothes as she turned in a slow circle. She was alone with no signs of man nor magic. She lowered herself to the ground, folding her legs beneath her.

Since her entrapment in a human body, Klavdiya had been unable to control her magic. But now, alone and away from everyone, she drew it towards her. Black tendrils snapped and popped as they curled around her human form. Her hairs stood on end and her jaw ached as she kept pulling on her magic. It was like a rebellious horse, trying to break free from its handler. She held tightly to the reins, even as they slipped through her fingers bit by bit.

Then, like a claustrophobic horse, her magic exploded from her grasp. It billowed out in a black cloud, sparks of silver and gold roiling inside.

Thunder roared. Dark, purple clouds rolled in, faster than they ought. Then came sheets of rain. Klavdiya gasped, suddenly soaked to the skin. To her left, the caravan's campfire spluttered and extinguished.

Digging her fingers into the softening mud, she focused on bringing the magic back to her. Again, it slithered over her body with crackles of black and silver. Still, it rebelled against her grip. She closed her fists around the mud, concentrating. An errant tendril snapped and broke away. A lightning bolt struck the earth dangerously close.

"Firebird," she whispered.

The brightness in her chest burned hotter. Gavriil wanted to live. He wanted to stay with her. All he needed was the firebird. No, just a feather. Then, he would not die. *I will still be with you.* She would not lose him. Not if she had anything to do with it.

Another lightning bolt struck the earth, this time ten or so paces away. She held tighter. She needed to find a trace of the firebird – no matter where the creature was. She and Gavriil could not waste away the rest of his life in Snegograd's wilderness. No, she would find him his firebird; he would be cured. Lightning struck again, so close that it singed her sleeve.

The next strike, she rolled, barely evading the burst of electricity. Her magic scattered away from her. She scrambled away from the large singe on the ground, wiping water out of her face. Slowly, the rain lessened, the thunder muted, and the lightning moved further off.

Her breathing ragged and her hands covered in mud, Klavdiya sat in the grass. Her own magic gave *her* bad luck. Rain. Thunder. Lightning that nearly killed her. She stared up at the sky, wishing she could take Baba Les's thick neck into her hands and twist. A *likho* was not subject to her own bad luck magic, just her victims. She glanced towards the caravan. They too were victims of her uncontrolled magic.

She hoped that Gavriil still slept and that no one noticed she was gone.

Klavdiya picked herself up, doing her best to rub the mud from her hands. The rain turned into a drizzle and the clouds above turned to a muted mauve. She trudged back towards the caravan, slicking her hair back and off her face.

A glimmer of light caught her eye. Turning away from the caravan, she looked towards the sky. Dipping in and out of the clouds was a ray of sunlight. She frowned. That could not be. It was the middle of the night, and the sun did not shine at night. The light dove out one of the clouds, and – her breath stuttering – she caught sight of it.

A gyr falcon spiraled downwards. No, not a gyr falcon. Gyr falcons were white and lightly speckled with brown. This falcon was as golden and shining as the sun with speckles that sparkled like red, orange, and yellow gemstones. The bird hooked upwards and back into the pale purple clouds, gleaming like sunrays. Then, once more, it dipped into view, fire streaking behind its wings as though the creature's feathers had lit the sky on fire.

CHAPTER 20

The Firebird

"I have found it." Klavdiya was sodden and hovering over him like a phantom in a ghost story.

Gavriil blinked – partially because he had just woken up and partially because he had no idea what she was talking about. "What did you find? And why are you wet?"

"I saw the firebird."

He did not register it at first. Then, slowly, the weight of what she had said pressed down on him. He could barely breathe, staring up at the carriage's upholstered ceiling. *The firebird.* The one thing left that might cure his blood miasma. But the Alkonost had predicted that finding the firebird would break him. He sat up, his arm brushing against Klavdiya's. He wasn't so fragile, not yet. He might not be broken.

And just as he had told Klavdiya: being broken was better than being dead. He took Klavdiya's hand. She was so cold, like touching an ice sculpture. Alive meant he could be with his wife, who despite his better judgment, he ... liked. He liked a lot.

He brought her hand to his chest, letting it rest above his heart. "Show me where it is, my lady."

They stepped outside into the drizzle. The air smelled of petrichor and fresh grass. The world was dark, clouds blotting out any starlight. Gavriil called for a guard to light a torch.

"There." Clutching his arm, Klavdiya pointed with her other hand towards the sky.

Behind a dark purple cloud, a flash of golden light blazed. It was nothing like the midnight sun but more like fire flying through the sky. Then, a golden gyr falcon, its wings sparkling with gemstones, dove towards the earth. Some two or so miles to the northeast, the grass lit in a blaze of fire that the drizzle dampened.

"Horses," Gavriil said to the nearest guard. "Now. And rouse the hunters. We have found the firebird."

The caravan woke in waves. The guards saddled horses, while the hunters grabbed their quivers and strung their bows. The servants brought waterproofed cloaks for the rain. His fingers laced with Klavdiya's, Gavriil stood at the northern edge of the camp, watching that guttering, golden light.

"My lord, my lady." A guard brought forward Gavriil's horse and the docile creature that was the only horse that tolerated Klavdiya.

Though his body ached, Gavriil knelt and laced his fingers, giving Klavdiya a leg up onto her mount. Then, he turned to his own mount and climbed into the saddle. The horse tossed its head in anticipation, jigging sideways, as though it knew the importance and the closeness of this goal. Shortening his reins, he squeezed his calves, urging the horse forward.

His body could not take a canter, his lack of sleep making his muscles weak, so they proceeded at a brisk trot across the landscape. Beside his mount, Klavdiya's horse jittered back and forth; the normally docile creature, for whatever reason, *hated* Klavdiya. To be fair, Klavdiya was not much of a horsewoman, clinging like a half-bird, half-lizard to the saddle and guiding the horse with harsh hands. Keeping one eye on his bride, Gavriil kept the glittering firebird directly between his horse's ears.

For fifteen minutes, Gavriil, Klavdiya, two guards, and two hunters trotted across the Snegogradian flatlands in the near-blackness. The rain misted down, coating them all in a fine spray. Gavriil's fingers went numb. Ahead, the firebird's fire spluttered and then went out.

His heart stopped for several beats. "Klavdiya, can you still sense it?"

"It's still in the grass," she said.

"Circle it," Gavriil ordered. "Bows ready."

He, Klavdiya, and one of the hunters turned right, while the other three made their way left around the spot where they had last seen the firebird. Quietly, Gavriil dismounted. He was no use hunting from the saddle. He grabbed the bow hanging from his saddle and strung it. He nocked an arrow.

Klavdiya slid from the saddle, her feet squelching in the grass.

The fiery falcon burst into the air, a rat between its talons. Gavriil's arrow flew wide. His hunters loosed their arrows. The firebird ducked and spun, evading both. Two more arrows sought the bird's heart, but the falcon dipped below them and then made for the sky, its wings beating firmly and steadily. His numb hands fumbling, Gavriil managed to nock another arrow and aim. But the bird was too high up.

The world spun around Gavriil as he watched the firebird fly away. A horrid, animalistic sound tore from his throat. His knees hit the ground. He tangled his fingers in his hair and then pulled. A golden beam vanishing into the darkness. His last hope soaring away on bejeweled wings.

"My lord." One of the guards came to his aid.

Klavdiya stood before him as still as stone, her skirts fluttering around her like dark petals. Gavriil's vision blurred. Rodú! Ignoring the guard, he crawled on hands and knees to her. Wrapping his arms around her legs, he buried his face in her skirts.

"Forgive me, my lady, I–" His voice broke. He swallowed, tried to compose himself. It was no use. "I don't want to leave you, Klavdiya. Rodú and all the gods of this earth know I would rather be broken than leave you behind."

She put her hands atop his head. She was trembling.

"I am scared of death," he murmured into her skirts. "Worse: I am scared I will never see you again. We could have had a future, something to look forward to."

"There must be another way," she said. "I will not let you die."

But there was nothing more. The firebird was gone, and it

would surely never let them get so close again. He tilted his face up to look at her. “Rodú, I wish I could be with you forever. I love you, Klavdiya Romanovna.”

CHAPTER 21

A Broken Curse

Klavdiya gasped and buckled. Gavriil caught her before she hit the ground. Black mist curled around her form – darker than even the starless night and colder than the depth of winter. She gripped the front of his caftan and mouthed something that he didn't understand. Then, she screamed, her body contorting. Black veins crawled beneath her skin like grim spiderwebs; and she spasmed.

"Klavdiya, my lady." Gavriil held her tight. He lifted his face to the guards. "Get the physician!"

The mist enveloped her body so that she looked like a woman made of swirling, black fog. He brushed the shadows away from her face. Her eye was watering. She felt so frail in his arms.

"Klavdiya, I love you," he said. "Help is coming."

Except what could a physician do for *this*?

A shadowy hand – no longer fingers but tendrils of cold night – cupped his face. So cold that it hurt. Her lips moved again, but no sound came out.

He clasped that strange appendage of tendrils, watching as the mist consumed his wife. Her skirt and legs turned into nothing more than shadowy tendrils – dozens of them. And the hand on his caftan was one thick tentacle. A single tear slipped out from Klavdiya's eye.

"Hold on," he prayed, holding her close even as she turned to nothing more than mist. "Hold on."

Though he brushed the dark mist away from her face again, it redoubled faster than his hand could work and smothered her.

Her body turned limp and slippery, her touch turning to nothing but the faintest whisper.

"Klavdiya, don't go," he murmured, clinging to her shadow until a wind drew what was left of his wife away. He felt as though his chest had been flayed open and carved out.

A foot away, the mist coalesced into a narrow silhouette. Then, a single black eye opened at the apex of the figure.

Gavriil choked on his own breath as his hunters staggered back. He opened his mouth to demand what this creature had done to his wife, but then he stared into the singular eye. Something was so deeply familiar about it that his heart started faintly beating again. "Y-you're Klavdiya."

The spirit dipped its "head" – if that is what he could call it.

"You're a *likho*."

Again, the spirit nodded.

Gavriil looked down at himself, looked at his arms which were still curved as though cradling his wife. But his wife... Could a *likho* marry a human? Klavdiya was not a *boyar*'s daughter. She was not a noblewoman. She wasn't even human. She was a bad luck spirit. Something twisted deep in his gut.

"You cursed me," he said.

Klavdiya stood utterly still.

"I could have caught the firebird." His throat hurt. His whole body hurt. "I could have caught the firebird. But you cursed me, you stopped me from catching it." He was shaking. "Do you realize I'm going to die?"

She hung her head.

He cradled his head in his hands, his whole body sagging. She looked contrite, but wouldn't a *likho* revel in misery? He hoped she had a shred of humanity, that she felt – if only just a little – some guilt. This wasn't just bad luck, this was a tragedy.

We will find the firebird.

I don't want you to die.

I will not let you die.

Those things she said, they were the words of a lover, of a wife. Or so Gavriil had thought. His shoulders curled forward over his chest. She was a *likho*, a spirit of misery and bad luck. She could not love. She could only bring grief. Certainly, she had only said such things to make this moment worse. He rubbed his arms; he felt painfully cold. He was a fool. She had utterly tricked him.

How could I not tell? *She had one eye!*

"Klavdiya," he began, "if that's your name."

She shivered forward anticipatorily.

"You must leave," he said. "I won't have you cursing me any more."

Is that how it worked? Gavriil hoped he could simply send her away. He could not bear to see his wife *whom he loved* – foolishly – turned into this creature. To stare at his own folly day after day. But the stories said that the harder you fought to rid yourself of a *likho*, the worse your luck got. Rodú, but he *had loved her*. He had loved a *likho* – just like that *vikhr* had said. Certainly, he had...

"I broke your curse," he said. "You have no power over me because I– I–" *I said I loved you.* He couldn't say it.

The *likho* bowed her head again. He was right.

"Go, then." Shakily, he stood, feeling as though the entire world pressed against his shoulders. "You're free."

She made a strange croaking noise and reached out a dark tendril.

Gavriil recoiled. "It's like the story: if I treat you well, you will leave me."

Klavdiya croaked again but did not extend a limb.

He started to shake, faced with this creature that had pretended to be his wife. That he had believed to be his wife. When he spoke, his voice was raw and louder than he meant. "Go wherever it is that a *likho* goes. Leave me be." When she didn't move, he shouted, "*Go!*"

The thing that was once Klavdiya trembled and stuttered backwards. Her single, black eye widened and looked wet. Gavriil stared back at her. What right did she have to look sad? She had tricked him. Her tendrils curled around themselves as though grasping at the air. Then, she dissipated like mist being blown away in the wind.

CHAPTER 22

A Thin Thread

The caravan avoided Snegograd as it snaked across the Ruthenian wilderness and back to Makovy. Springtime was bowing out, and summer came on stage. The grass turned emerald green; the barley and rye fields grew gold; and the berries burst like sapphires and rubies. The world was happy.

Gavriil, however, was sick. Sicker than he had ever been. It was as though losing Klavdiya had sapped him of some essential life force. Most days, he was feverish with skin that was hot to the touch, though he felt painfully cold. He slaked his constant thirst with *kvass* and fruitwine, feeling lightheaded from either drunkenness or the blood miasma – he couldn't tell. He spent much of his day in bed or in his sitting room, looking out the window at the garden. He was most often visited by his physician. And Mikhail Petrovich.

You told me so, he had told Mikhail. *There was something wrong with her. Not a spy, though, a spirit.*

Half-awake, Gavriil sat in the sitting room one day with a carafe of fruitwine and a dish of fresh chokeberries near his elbow. A maid came in, brushing away the non-existent dust. He blinked a few times and then recognized her. Elvira, Klavdiya's lady's maid.

"Did you know what she was?" he asked, his voice ragged.

Elvira dipped into a curtsy. "No, my lord. But she was an interesting *boyarynya*."

"How so?" His gaze drifted to the window and down to the garden where Klavdiya had claimed a *vodnik* lived in the pond.

"She was always asking me how to make you love her, my

lord," the maid said. "She seemed so earnest. It's strange to think ... that she was what she was."

Gavriil nodded. Part of him still didn't believe that his sweet, one-eyed bride had been a *likho* in disguise. But then he remembered the ominous omen and the broken mirror at his wedding, the broken carriage wheels, the cracked windows. They weren't all coincidences – like he had told himself – but the workings of a *likho*. What he didn't know was if Klavdiya did it on purpose or if misfortune followed her simply because of what she was.

"You have that rash again, my lord," the maid said. "Shall I send for the physician?"

"She'll come on her own soon enough," Gavriil said. "You may leave."

Elvira curtsied again and scurried out; and then Gavriil was alone again.

For the most part, he preferred aloneness. It was quiet and he could think. Or not think, if he so desired. So, he dozed while sitting upright, dreaming of a one-eyed shadow that crept through a grand forest. The shadow stalked a golden bird that fluttered just out of view. The shadow reached out tentacles, ready to encircle the bird. But then the golden bird would swoop out of reach. The shadow snapped its tentacles back to its side and croaked in frustration. Watching the scene, Gavriil felt very sad.

He woke sometime later with a terrible kink in his neck and dry eyes.

The physician was there, sluicing water over his forehead. She was a plump woman with golden hair that she kept in two braids, one over each shoulder. On her left breast, she wore a pin with the symbol of the goddess Zorya – who was the goddess of both war and healing. A Zorya's Order-trained physician was rare in these areas, but Gavriil was lucky to have her. She had kept him alive this long, which was longer than anyone expected.

"I don't like your fevers," she said.

"I don't either," he said.

She scowled. "I've made an anti-fever tisane as well as your usual anti-miasma paste."

Gavriil took the steaming cup of anti-fever medication. It was earthy-green in color and smelled like willow and ginger. He drank it in two quick gulps. His stomach twisted in rebellion, but he managed to keep it down. The medication for miasma went down easier; he was used to its taste and consistency by now.

"I am still waiting for a response from Zorya's Order," the physician said, taking the empty cups back. "We can hope they have another solution to the blood miasma."

Gavriil raised his eyebrows. Zorya's Order had already recommended the firebird feather. He could not imagine what could be more esoteric, more challenging to find than that.

She pressed her lips into a thin line. "Hopefully, something that does not move. A plant of some sort."

"I have already written and stamped my will," Gavriil said. "And I have sent for my cousin. She will make a fine *boyarynya* when I am gone."

"You have months," the physician insisted. "I'll make sure of it, my lord. You do not need to plan for the end. Not yet."

"Your treatments have kept me alive far longer than either of us predicted," he said. "But I am getting weaker each day. At the very least, I can have all my affairs in order and have my cousin near to help me manage the estate as my condition declines."

"Of course, my lord." The physician nodded. "And know this: I will be loyal to you until your last breath. My allegiance will not change until the birds carry your soul on to the next world."

"I'm honored."

Mikhail, the steward, the cook, the footman, and his manservant had told him much the same. None, it seemed, wanted a new *boyar* – or *boyarynya* – in Makovy. Gavriil wished that he could stay, that he could lead Makovy for another four or more decades, that he would die quietly of old age. But Rodú did not offer him that fate. The thread of Gavriil's life grew thinner and thinner. Soon enough, it would snap and he would be done.

CHAPTER 23

A Grimoire

Klavdiya floated through Snegograd's wilds. For a while, she told herself that she was searching for the firebird again. Then, she decided to go back to her usual behavior as a *likho* and find a victim. She hung around a serf for a couple of weeks, making him particularly clumsy and prone to dropping things. However, these antics did not bring her delight like they once had. So, eventually, she let the serf go and began wandering again. She was like a wisp of smoke blown away on the wind.

She found Snegograd's manor and took shelter in the courtyard, where the *dvorovik* tolerated her.

A few days after she arrived, the catlike creature with eyes that bulged like a frog's came waddling up, leaning heavily on a cane that was carved to resemble a bull. "I don't normally let *likho* stay. They bring too much chaos."

Klavdiya picked herself off the ground and dusted herself off, expecting to be thrown out. After all that time in her human body, she now felt weird being mostly shadow and tentacles. Her movements were awkward.

"But you look pathetic," the *dvorovik* said, gesturing with his cane. "You don't look like you'll be causing any mischief, will you?"

Klavdiya closed her eye and shook her head.

"Good," he harrumphed.

"Wait," she said before he tottered off. "Do the people here know what happened to Klavdiya Romanovna?"

The *dvorovik* narrowed his eyes. "The lord and lady think she still lives with her husband in Makovy. We spirits know that she said the prayer to Baba Les and was transported to the witch's house, instead of going to Makovy."

Klavdiya narrowed her eye and leaned in. "There is a prayer to Baba Les?"

"The humans have it in a book in the manor." The *dvorovik* frowned. "If I could guess, I'd say it was demonic."

She tilted her head as an idea began to form. "But it brings the speaker to Baba Les? She's a *ved'ma*, not a demon."

The *dvorovik* snorted. "It's all the same to me. Blasted human stuff."

Long after the *dvorovik* had left her to her own devices, Klavdiya considered the possibility of a prayer or a spell that could bring her directly to Baba Les. She had never thought she would want to see the witch again. But Baba Les had more secrets than a bird had feathers, and maybe the witch would be willing to share one with Klavdiya. The *likho* drifted back and forth listlessly in the courtyard. Would Baba Les trap her again? Or would the witch agree to bargain? Klavdiya's plan would not work if the witch chose the former.

After crossing the courtyard for the umpteenth time, she finally decided to chance another encounter with Baba Les. Even if there was a small chance Klavdiya got what she wanted from the witch, the risk was worth it.

But first, she needed to find the spell that the original Klavdiya Romanovna had used.

It took some cajoling and convincing, but the *dvorovik* finally allowed her to cling to the back of one of the scullions. The boy ended up tripping and dropping the iron pot he was carrying, breaking the toes on his right foot, but Klavdiya was inside the manor. She released the boy and floated away.

She slithered from room to room to room. The manor was much larger than she remembered from her time being human. She slunk through the larder, the buttery, the kitchen. She skimmed the ceiling of the great hall and many of the vaulted corridors. She found bedrooms and studies, and even the chapel. For all the space, there were very few people in Snegograd, leaving the many rooms empty.

Finally, she found a small room with a desk in the center and bookshelves lining the walls. The place had, seemingly, been long abandoned because no candles remained in the sconces; and a thick layer of dust covered everything. Footprints walked through that dust and there was a thick smear on one of the shelves. Floating closer to that shelf, Klavdiya read the spines on the books, each one written in an elegant and curling hand.

Wrapping her tendrils around the least dusty of the books, she pulled it off the shelf. *The Malachite Girl and Other Stories.* Klavdiya let her tendrils clean the dust from its cover. The binding was pigskin dyed a sickly-looking green; and the textblock had been painted gold.

Carefully, she parted the pages of the book. Inside, the pages were illuminated in red, gold, and blue. And there were paintings as well. She found herself staring at a girl of perhaps fourteen wearing a dress made of malachite stone. Squinting, she turned the pages until she finally found a story about a girl whose jealous stepsisters sent her out into the woods, where she was taken in by an old witch. Her tendrils curled across the parchment, following the words across the page.

There. Beneath the picture of a house on stilts was a short rhyme. And below that were runes.

Klavdiya held up one of her tendrils where faint, coal-gray scars still marked where Baba Les had carved the rune. Though runes came from nature and from the spirits, but the *ved'ma* had become experts in twisting runes' power to their will. Klavdiya suspected that this book was not just a collection of fairytales but a witch's grimoire – though she did not have one inkling as to whom the grimoire might belong to.

Nor did it matter, so long as she could reach Baba Les.

Klavdiya said the rhyme and traced the runes.

CHAPTER 24

Magic and Misfortune

Gavriil woke from a dream that he could not remember. He laid in bed, wrapped in several layers of blankets, with an impossible-to-kick shiver. He turned over. The curtains were open, letting the full moon pour into the center of the room. The rest was an impenetrable shadow. Letting his eyes adjust to the contrast of moonlight and pure darkness, he realized: the window was broken, its glass cracked in a spidery pattern. He sluggishly propped himself up on an elbow. The window hadn't been broken when he went to sleep.

"Gavriil."

He nearly fell out of bed, he startled so strongly. "Klavdiya."

She materialized out of the shadows, her clothes simple and tar-black. Her skin shimmered silvery in the moonlight; and her hair fell like swirling ink down to her waist. She wore no eyepatch, and shadows collected in the divot where her eye should be.

"I told you to leave me." He reached for the dagger that he kept tucked between the bedframe and the wall. Then, he hesitated. "Wait, the last time I saw you, you were a *likho*."

Now, she was decidedly human. The form he recognized. The form he loved, despite himself.

"I gave up my magic."

He glanced to the broken window. *Not quite*. "Why?"

She rummaged in her sleeve. "In exchange for this."

She withdrew a golden, glowing feather that lit the room like a torch. She met his gaze across the room, and Gavriil's world spun.

"A firebird feather." He blinked several times, half-doubting his own eyes. But the golden feather remained in her hand like a beacon. "What–? How–?" He shook his head and took a deep breath. "Start from the very beginning. Why did a *likho* marry me? And why is she bringing me a firebird feather now?"

Klavdiya told a story of being trapped by a powerful *ved'ma* and taking a bargain in hopes she could escape the *ved'ma* and become a *likho* again. The catch? She had to marry and make her new husband love her. He marveled at how similar the situation was to the fairytale version of the *likho* – where the man who treated his *likho* well was able to be rid of her.

"Maybe I should have told you that I loved you sooner," he said.

She moved closer. "You needed me to find the firebird."

"But we lost it."

She lay the feather on the bed beside him. "We don't have the bird, but we have the feather."

He touched the glowing feather gingerly. It was warm like a candle flame. "You haven't finished your story. How did you get this feather?"

"After I turned back into a *likho*, I found my way back to Baba Les," Klavdiya said. "She has *everything* in her house and she is a powerful *ved'ma*. If anyone would have a firebird feather, it would be here. And if she did not have a firebird feather, she would have another cure."

"You did not need to keep searching for the cure." Gavriil slumped against the pillows and then took the feather in his hands. He cradled it against his chest. "Even I had given up."

She did not acknowledge what he said. Instead, she continued her story. "I used a human spellbook to find Baba Les, and I asked to make another bargain. I wanted a firebird feather. She offered to give me a firebird feather in exchange for my magic."

"You are a spirit," Gavriil said. "You are *all* magic. What is left when your magic is taken away?"

"I thought I would die," Klavdiya said. "But perhaps I became part human while with you. Because beneath my magic and misfortune, there was this human body. Baba Les took my magic and put it in a jar. I became human. And then, I was given the firebird feather."

"Why?" he asked. "I had repudiated you. And ... and you are – were – a spirit with magic and free agency. Why would you give that up to try to save me?"

She reached forward, her fingertips brushing the back of his hand and sending a trill of heat through him. "An eternity knowing that you died is worse than a short life knowing that you lived." She was quiet for a long moment. Then, she said, almost inaudibly, "I love you. I would die so that you could live."

He caught her hand and kissed her knuckles. "I love you, too, Klavdiya. I don't even care that you are – were – a *likho*. You've never been anything but good luck to me."

She sat on the edge of the bed and embraced him. He wrapped his arms around her. The firebird feather glowed hot between their hearts. He kissed her hair and her ear, his hands stroking down her back. No longer did she feel peculiarly cold. Instead, she was warm and soft; and she melded against him. He could stay like this forever.

ABOUT THE AUTHOR

Rebecca Ganesh

Rebecca Ganesh is the author and cover designer for the new romantasy series the Ruthenian Chronicle.

A professionally trained librarian, Rebecca spends their time gathering all the most compelling and erudite information to make their characters and world building pop.

Rebecca enjoys a good fantasy novel and is always on the lookout for new story ideas.

Get freebies, book recommendations, and behind-the-scenes looks at: https://rebeccaganesh.com.

THE RUTHENIAN CHRONICLE

The Ruthenian Chronicle is a romantasy series of novellas, each centered on a different couple and based on Slavic folklore. These books can be read in any order and you don't necessarily have to read them all.

The Bone Doll

Real heroes are made of blood and scars and wounds so deep you cannot see them.

Viktor needs to bring back magic that can control the raging forest spirit that threatens to tear down his family's estate. He learns of a bone carving that can bind spirits, he sets out to find it. When he finally finds the talisman – the Bone Doll – out on the eastern tundra, he learns that it can only be used by its bearer - a grumpy shaman named Syra who only begrudgingly agrees to help him.

Traveling southward with the nobleman Viktor, Syra finds herself away from home for the first time, carrying a talisman that may or may not be cursed. And to make matters worse, she doesn't know if her magic is strong enough to wield the Bone Doll and defeat the forest spirit.

As they navigate wilderness and civilization, the mundane and the magical, Syra and Viktor's feelings grow and change. But Viktor hasn't been entirely honest about this quest: this is a journey from which Syra won't return.

The Wooden Heart

"I would have never thought that a wooden heart would beat."
"Only for you."

Having settled affairs with his estate, Viktor returns to the tundra and to Syra. However, his and Syra's hopes for a long-term partnership and romance are jeopardized. Viktor reveals that he has been cursed by the vengeful forest spirit that had threatened to destroy his estate. He is turning into wood. Syra devises a plan to visit a magical island with ancient and powerful spirits who may be able to break the curse.

Will Syra and Viktor make it to the island before Viktor turns completely to wood? Will the spirits remove the curse? Or will the spirits demand too steep a price?

Perfect for readers who loved The Witcher, Spinning Silver, The Wolf & the Woodsman, and The Bear & the Nightingale who want a little more romance.

This short short story follow the events in The Bone Doll.

The Malachite Maze

He had always had a soft spot for her, even before he knew that a boy could love a girl.

In prison for murdering her husband, Masha is certain that she will be sold to a slaver and shipped off to a foreign land to live her days in servitude. So when the jailer comes to get her, she is surprised that the white-blonde, broad-shouldered warrior who has paid her bail is not a slaver but her ex-best friend Dir - a man whose heart she broke years ago.

Dir needs Masha's help in looking for a magical crown. The Princess of Vecherny is offering a large sum of money to whoever finds the crown; and Dir wants to pay his way out of poverty.

And if Masha doesn't help him find the crown, Dir will reveal Masha's closest-held secret - a secret even more dangerous than murder.

The One Eyed Bride

"An eternity knowing that you died is worse than a short life knowing that you lived."

Klavdiya is a likho, a spirit that causes bad luck, that has been trapped into an eternity of servitude by a witch. When a fleeing bride comes to the witch for help, Klavdiya is given an opportunity for freedom. The catch? She must make the jilted bridegroom love her.

Gavriil is dying. He marries the daughter of another powerful boyar in order to obtain the right to hunt the near-mythic firebirds, hoping their magical feathers hold the cure. He finds his new bride, however, not quite what he was expecting.

As Gavriil hunts for a cure and Klavdiya hunts for her freedom, will they find love? Or will their luck run out?

www.ingramcontent.com/pod-product-compliance
Lightning Source LLC
LaVergne TN
LVHW011047110826
845149LV00015B/3395

* 9 7 9 8 9 9 9 7 6 7 9 5 0 *